BEST.
NIGHT.
EVER.

CHECK OUT OTHER BOOKS BY THE AUTHORS OF **BEST. NIGHT. EVER.**

Rachele Alpine
Operation Pucker Up
You Throw Like a Girl

Ronni Arno
Ruby Reinvented
Dear Poppy
Coming soon:
Molly in the Middle

Alison Cherry
The Classy Crooks Club
Willows vs. Wolverines

Stephanie Faris
30 Days of No Gossip
25 Roses

Jen Malone
At Your Service
The Sleepover
Coming soon:
The Art of the Swap

Gail Nall
Breaking the Ice
Out of Tune

Jen Malone and Gail Nall
You're Invited
You're Invited Too

Dee Romito
The BFF Bucket List
Coming soon:
No Place Like Home

BEST.
NIGHT.
EVER.

A STORY TOLD FROM SEVEN POINTS OF VIEW

RACHELE ALPINE
RONNI ARNO | ALISON CHERRY
STEPHANIE FARIS | JEN MALONE
GAIL NALL | DEE ROMITO

ALADDIN
NEW YORK LONDON TORONTO SYDNEY NEW DELHI

ALADDIN

An imprint of Simon & Schuster Children's Publishing Division
1230 Avenue of the Americas, New York, New York 10020
First Aladdin hardcover edition August 2017
Text compilation and "Ashlyn" copyright © 2017 by Jennifer Malone
"Carmen" copyright © 2017 by Rachele Alpine
"Ellie" copyright © 2017 by Ronni Arno
"Genevieve" copyright © 2017 by Alison Cherry
"Ryan" copyright © 2017 by Stephanie Faris
"Tess" copyright © 2017 by Gail Nall
"Jade" copyright © 2017 by Dee Romito
Jacket illustration copyright © 2017 by James Lopez
All rights reserved, including the right of reproduction in whole or in part in any form.
ALADDIN and related logo are registered trademarks of Simon & Schuster, Inc.
For information about special discounts for bulk purchases, please contact
Simon & Schuster Special Sales at 1-866-506-1949 or business@simonandschuster.com.
The Simon & Schuster Speakers Bureau can bring authors to your live event.
For more information or to book an event contact the Simon & Schuster Speakers Bureau
at 1-866-248-3049 or visit our website at www.simonspeakers.com.
Jacket designed by Karin Paprocki
Interior designed by Mike Rosamilia
The text of this book was set in Adobe Garamond Pro.
Manufactured in the United States of America 0818 FFG
4 6 8 10 9 7 5 3
This book has been cataloged with the Library of Congress.
ISBN 978-1-4814-8660-6 (hc)
ISBN 978-1-4814-8662-0 (eBook)

DEDICATED TO
ALL THOSE WHO BRAVE
MIDDLE SCHOOL DANCES,
ESPECIALLY THE FRIENDS
WHO BRAVED OURS WITH US.

BEST.
NIGHT.
EVER.

CARMEN { 6:00 P.M. }

USUALLY LYNNFIELD MIDDLE SCHOOL'S gym smells like sweaty socks and armpits.

But tonight, everything is different.

Tonight, the gym smells like perfume, hairspray, and the pizza that everyone devoured right away. And instead of getting pelted in the face during a vicious game of dodgeball or doing a million jumping jacks, my friends and I are about to make history when we perform our band's hit song, "Hear Us Roar."

The room buzzes with excitement. Our classmates gather at the makeshift stage the drama club constructed, some pushing to get as close as possible, others taking selfies in front of the giant sign the decorating committee hung up with our name, Heart Grenade, written across it.

Suddenly the room goes dark and the audience erupts in cheers. This is it. Our moment!

A single spotlight turns on, illuminating me.

I look out into the crowd and soak up the moment as my classmates' shouts wash over me. I picture myself as they might. My long black hair is flat-ironed sleek and shiny, and the light from above draws attention to my red streaks. My satin dress poofs out at the bottom, and the short white leather jacket looks amazing over it. I have on Mom's vintage biker boots with the big silver buckles, and hot pink tights add the perfect touch. I'm rocker cute, as my best friend, Tess, likes to say.

"Hello, Lynnfield Middle School!" I yell into the microphone. The sound of my voice sweeps through the gym. "We're Heart Grenade, and we're ready to rock!"

Tess starts playing the drums, Faith comes in on the bass, and as Claudia launches into her signature guitar riff, the lights go up over the whole band, and our classmates go wild.

I open my mouth to start singing . . . and something soft smacks me in the head.

"Ouch!"

And just like that I'm jolted out of the best daydream ever and back into the worst reality ever. Because instead of being in the middle school gym performing with Heart Grenade like I'm supposed to be tonight, I'm surrounded by beige-and-maroon-striped wallpaper in a very tiny and very crowded hotel room with my family.

My eyes land on my ten-year-old brother, Lucas. He's dressed in a gray suit that's too short for him, and his dark hair is all spiky, even though Mom told him it would be really nice if he just combed it straight. But his appearance isn't what I care about; it's what is in his hands. He's holding Pandy, my bear that I *may* still sleep with, although I'd never admit that to anyone. He dances around me and dangles Pandy in front of my face.

I yank her away from him. "Get your grubby hands off of my bear."

"Gladly. I've got some reading to do anyway." Lucas pulls my diary from under his pillow on the bed.

"Give me that!" I reach to grab the notebook with the hand that isn't holding Pandy, but he pulls it away from me. I have no idea how the little sneak got hold of it, since I packed it deep down into my duffel bag, but there's no way I'm letting him see what's inside. He'd never let me live down the pages I filled about how cute my bandmate Claudia's brother is.

"Mooooom," I yell, but she waves a hand at me. She's talking on the phone in rapid-fire Spanish to my aunt Sonia, or "the mother of the bride," as everyone keeps saying, and is trying to convince her that something to do with the flowers is going to be all right. But meanwhile, this diary situation most certainly is not going to turn out all right.

I tackle Lucas and thankfully wrestle the notebook away from him, but not before getting an elbow to the gut and a knee to my head.

"You'd better sleep with one eye open," I warn him. "I'm not going to forget this."

"Ohhhh, I'm so scared," he replies and rolls his eyes.

"You look like Christmas," my seven-year-old brother, Alex, says, and my attention shifts to him. Yep, I have two younger brothers. Two *annoying* little brothers. It's pretty much the worst ever.

"Christmas?" This is March; that holiday is long gone.

"Yep, with that green dress and those awful red streaks you put in your hair, you make me want to watch *Rudolph* and hang ornaments on the tree."

"Whatever! You're the ridiculous one, with your purple tie and sweater vest," I say.

"If you say so, Jolly Old Saint Nick."

"I don't look like Christmas," I tell him, but I walk over to the mirror. The girl who stares back at me isn't happy at all. Instead of the cute black dress I gazed at every time we went to the mall, the one I'd planned to buy for our big concert, I have on a junior bridesmaid dress that's about as pretty as a pillowcase. It's made of some stretchy fabric that bunches up around my waist and digs into my armpits. And it's green. Not the cute emerald green or Kelly green that all the celebrities wear these days, but bright elf green. My brothers are right; with the red streaks in my hair, I'm ready to deck the halls and have myself a merry little Christmas.

"I'm suddenly in the mood for milk and cookies," Lucas says, coming up behind me.

"That's it," I announce. "I refuse to wear this!"

I go to my suitcase and pull out my jeans with the rhine-stones that I wore on the drive here because right now, no dress is better than wearing this one. I try to reach behind and unzip the offending dress, so I'll at least look the part of the lead singer even if I'm not rocking out with everyone back at school.

"Not a chance," Mom says. The phone is still up against

her ear, so I pray maybe she's talking to my aunt instead of me. "You're not putting that on," she says, crushing all my hopes.

"But why not? The ceremony is over, and we took a million pictures of me in this awful thing. Can't I wear these now?"

"You're wearing the dress your cousin picked out for you. It's your cousin's night, so you'll do what makes her happy."

What about what makes me *happy? It was supposed to be my night,* I want to say, but it's no use trying to convince Mom. I can tell from the glare she gives me that I won't win this argument.

I try a different approach and decide to talk to Dad instead. He's always the easier one to convince, especially when it involves ice cream before dinner or staying up past my bedtime. Dad's a sucker for my sad face, and sticking out my bottom lip and looking especially pathetic always seals the deal.

I've studied the bus maps, and even though we are almost three hours from home, if I take the six thirty p.m. bus, I might make it back so I can sing with the band. Imagine everyone's surprise and delight if I showed up. They'd be so excited, especially since they were all upset when I broke the news that my parents were making me go to this wedding. It was awful; we all cried a little bit. Well, except Genevieve, who got really, really quiet. She's probably thrilled to be in the spotlight since she only joined a month ago as a backup singer and now she gets to take my spot in the lead.

"Dad, what do you think about taking me to the bus station before you all go to the reception? I can go home early, sing with the band, and stay with Tess."

"Yeah, and he can also drop me off at the airport for a flight to Disney World," Alex says, and I want to scream. "There's no way you're going to be allowed to ride the bus alone."

"Stay out of this," I snap.

"He's right," Dad says. He doesn't even take his eyes off the TV, and I can't believe he's abandoning me instead of being my ally. "That's too dangerous. And besides, you know how excited Mom is for us to spend family time together."

"This is so unfair. It's Heart Grenade's big night. We worked so hard to win the Battle of the Bands at the mall, and now I can't claim our prize."

"We've been over this already, Carmen. You made a commitment to be in your cousin's wedding," Mom says. She's finally hung up the phone, probably so she can direct all her attention toward continuing to ruin my night.

"But that was before we won." I try to reason with her. "When am I ever going to be on TV again?"

"You'll survive," Mom says.

But I'm really not sure I will. Our local station is broadcasting Heart Grenade's concert to everyone during the evening news, and I won't be a part of it.

"You don't understand. Anyone could be watching. I'm pretty sure Taylor Swift got discovered in a similar way."

"And I also bet that she went to all her family weddings," Mom says. She touches up her bright red lipstick in the mirror and doesn't seem to care at all that my life is ending. "It's good to spend time as a family."

"Well, you got your wish," I say.

"How about you try to have fun? You might even find that being at this wedding isn't so awful, *mi pajarita*."

She tries to pull me into a hug that I most definitely do not want.

I wiggle out of it and back away. "Fun? You don't understand anything! When I have daughters, I'm always going to listen to them and make sure I support everything they want to do."

I huff and puff all the way to the bathroom to make sure everyone knows how mad I am. I slam the door and sit on the edge of the bathtub.

This is a million times more horrible than I'd imagined. I pull out my cell phone and send a text to Tess.

Help! Emergency! Come save me STAT!!! This is a tragedy! I need to be with all of you!

I wait for her to reply and wish that she really could come to save me. But when you're stuck an entire state away in a hotel room, that's pretty much impossible.

Someone bangs on the door.

"Time's up, Mrs. Claus. I need to get in there," Alex yells.

I turn on the water in the tub full blast to drown him out, scroll through my Instagram feed, and torture myself with picture after picture of everyone getting ready for the dance. I burst out laughing at a picture from earlier in the afternoon of my classmate (and Tess's mortal enemy) Mariah with a green face mask on and the caption, *Do you all like my makeup for the dance? Perfect, right?!* I scroll through and pause on a cartoon one of my classmates drew of Heart Grenade's logo. *Can't wait to hear my favorite band live* is written on the bottom.

"My life is over!" I wail.

"Carmen, open up right now! This isn't funny," Lucas whines. "I drank two cans of soda and need to use the bath-room."

"Should've thought about that before you made fun of my dress."

I hear Dad yell something with my name in it, so I know it's only a matter of time before he comes over and tells me to open the door.

I grab for my phone as it lights up, telling me I have a text.

Except it isn't from Tess.

It's from Genevieve.

THE Genevieve, who is taking my place tonight as lead singer. A.k.a. . . . the last person in the world I want to hear from.

Hope the wedding is fun. Wish you were here!

I feel a little better. At least the band is thinking of me.

I'm about to respond when another message from her pops up on the screen.

Any last-minute advice?

Seriously? She's asking me for advice? That's like kicking someone when they're down.

I don't want to give her advice; I want to be up there onstage. I fight back tears while Lucas continues to pound on the door and Alex sings Christmas carols. And his song choice couldn't be better, because it's going to be a "Silent Night" for me as the lead singer of Heart Grenade.

GENEVIEVE { **6:31 P.M.** }

IT'S MY FIRST NIGHT AS THE LEAD SINGER OF
Heart Grenade. And if I have anything to say about it, it'll
also be my last.

I've always loved to sing. I still love to sing. The thing is,
I only love to *perform* if I'm in the background or part of a
group, where my voice can blend with everyone else's. When
I sing at church or in select choir at school, it's impossible
to pick individual voices apart, so I'm able to squash down
the panic that tries to claw its way up from my stomach
every time I step onto a stage. But just the thought of being
pinned alone in a bright white spotlight like a spider trapped

under a plastic cup is enough to make me feel sick.

Why does Carmen's cousin have to get married *today* of all days? And what was I *thinking* when I told the band I'd fill in as lead singer? I should've told them I wasn't ready for this. But none of the Heart Grenade girls know me very well yet—I only joined the band last month, after they kicked out their last backup singer for skipping too many rehearsals—and I was afraid they'd drop me, too, if I said no. Then again, they'll probably throw me out anyway if I mess up tonight for them.

I figure maybe I'll feel more confident if I at least look like the lead singer I'm supposed to be, so I change into the outfit my best friend, Sydney, helped me pick out. Shimmery silver tank top. Leopard-print skirt with tulle underneath, a hand-me-down from my cousin. Lime green jacket. Glittery black tights. I top it all off with my lucky green Chuck Taylor high-tops.

I am a rock star, I think to myself. But when I look in the mirror, I can't totally tell whether this look says *rock star* or *victim of a fabric store explosion*. Syd will be able to help when she gets here. She's really into fashion blogs all of a sudden.

There's a knock on my bedroom door. "Gen?" Papa calls. "You dressed?"

"Yeah." My dads come in, and I spin around to show off my outfit. "Too much?"

"Definitely not. You look great," Dad says. Then again, I'm not positive he's the best judge. His shirt is such a vivid shade of orange that it almost hurts to look at it, and he's not even dressed up for a special occasion. All he's doing tonight is watching TV with Papa.

A little shiver of fear zings up my spine when I remember that one of the things they'll be watching is *me*. They wanted to come to school and see my performance live, but I told them it would be much cooler to see me on TV. Really, it's mostly because I don't want to see their faces fall if I completely freeze up.

"Want me to do a zigzag braid for you?" Papa asks, and I nod. He's amazingly good with hair for someone who shaves his head. Sydney always tries to do cool stuff with my mass of wild curls, but she can never wrestle them into submission the way Papa can. Syd's hair is the complete opposite of mine: blond and soft and stick straight.

I sit down on the floor, and Papa perches behind me on the bed and starts braiding. The movement of his fingers against my head is soothing. "How're you feeling about tonight?" he asks.

I've never told Dad and Papa how scared performing

makes me—I don't want them to know I'm not brave like they are. They're in this amazing gay men's chorus, and both of them sing lead all the time. Neither of them has any idea I was offered a solo in this spring's choir concert and turned it down because I was terrified. They think I auditioned for Heart Grenade because I wanted to try singing a different kind of music, not because I thought it might help me get comfortable singing in smaller groups.

So I try to shove all my panic to the very bottom of my stomach before I shrug and say, "I feel okay, I guess."

Dad must hear the tiny shake in my voice, because he reaches over and rubs my shoulder. "You're going to be wonderful. I'm so excited for you."

"Carmen did a great job at the Battle of the Bands, but I think you have a better voice," Papa says. "I heard you practicing in the shower yesterday, and you sounded spectacular."

I know he's trying to boost my confidence, and I love him for it. But the thing is, it doesn't really matter which of us sounds better. Carmen can handle the pressure of being a lead singer, and I can't.

"Thanks," I say anyway. I'm glad I'm facing away from him so I don't have to force a smile.

"If you want to practice your song again, we're happy to listen," Papa says.

"That's okay. Syd said I can sing it for her one more time before we go."

As if I've summoned her, the doorbell rings, and knowing my best friend is outside makes me feel a little calmer. Papa snaps an elastic onto the ends of my hair. "All done. You want to get the door?"

"Yup." I get up. "Thanks for the braid."

"I can do your makeup, too, if you want."

"No thanks," I call back as I jog down the stairs. The last time I asked him to help me with that, he used way too much, and I ended up looking like Grandma Evelyn.

I pull the door open, and I'm already saying, "Oh man, I'm so glad you're here . . ." before I register what I'm seeing.

Sydney's on my doorstep, a dress bag slung over her shoulder. But there are three other girls crowded behind her: Abby from our class, and Shanti and Ilana from Ms. Crowley's class. It's not like I didn't know Syd was friends with them—I've seen pictures of them together on Instagram, and Shanti and Ilana sit at our lunch table sometimes. Syd has never ditched me for them or anything, so it didn't bother me that they hung out. But tonight is our first dance ever, not to mention my first big solo performance, and it was supposed to be just us. It's always been just us for everything important.

"Hey, Gen!" Syd's voice sounds a little too loud and breathy, and when she throws her arms around me, her dress bag crunches and crinkles against my shoulder. "I told the girls they could get ready here too. I hope that's okay."

It's not okay. I'm so nervous right now that I can barely keep it together in front of Syd and my parents, and she definitely should've asked if she could bring other people to *my house*. But it's too late now. It's not like I can refuse to let them in.

"Um," I say, because that's all my brain can handle.

Syd takes that as a yes. "Come on," she says to the other girls, and everyone tromps through the door with their dresses and bags, making the foyer feel way too crowded. Syd has always treated my house and my family like they belong to her, too, but this is the first time I've ever minded. Usually it makes me feel like we're sisters.

"Your place is really nice," Abby says.

My dads appear at the top of the stairs, and their eyes widen when they see how many people are here. I'm half hoping they'll freak out and send everyone home, but they don't. Dad just says, "Hi, Sydney. Who are your other friends, Gen?"

Syd acts like the question was directed at her and introduces everyone, and all the girls smile politely and say hi. "Come on up," Papa says. "We'll stay out of your way, but let us know if you need anything, okay?"

"Thanks, Mr. Brooks!" Sydney chirps, and all four of them head up the stairs and around the corner to my room. I take a couple of deep breaths—*I can do this, I can handle this*—and then I follow.

My room is already covered with their stuff by the time I get there. There are dress bags and jackets heaped on my bed, a duffel bag on my chair, a curling iron on my desk, and shoes scattered all over the floor, so I hover awkwardly in the doorway. Abby and Shanti are huddled together, giggling over something on Abby's phone, and Ilana's chattering on and on about hair-curling techniques. Six months ago, Syd would've rolled her eyes and made a face at me over Ilana's shoulder, but now she looks superinterested. These days, it's getting harder and harder to find my best friend in her.

Ilana spots me and takes in my outfit, head to toe and back again. "Is that what you're wearing?" she asks.

"Yeah?" I don't intend for it to be a question, but it comes out like one—I can't tell if she's saying that my outfit is wrong. I smooth the leopard-print skirt with both hands. "Syd picked it out."

"I think it's perfect," Syd says. "Very punk rock." But all the girls are pulling their dresses out of the bags now, and even though they don't match or anything, all of them are satiny and pastel and delicate with tiny spaghetti straps. It looks like maybe they came from the same store. When Syd didn't ask me to go to the mall with her, I'd assumed she was wearing something she already had, not shopping with other people.

I look down at my Chucks and wonder if punk rock is really what I want to be when everyone else's outfit is so classy and feminine.

"Your hair looks cool," says Shanti. "Did you do it yourself?"

"No, my dad did it."

Abby unzips her jeans and wriggles out of them; she doesn't seem self-conscious at all about taking her clothes off in front of me, even though we're not friends. "Which one is your real dad?"

I *hate* when people ask me that. My skin is almost an exact midpoint between Dad's pale skin and Papa's dark brown, so I could be biologically related to either of them. But come on— it's nobody's business.

"They're both real," I say, misunderstanding on purpose.

A satisfying blush tints Abby's cheeks pink. "No, but, I mean . . . which one is, like, your *dad* dad?"

"She's adopted," Sydney says. "Can I borrow your lipstick?"

I hate that my best friend is explaining my family like I can't speak for myself, like it needs to be explained at all. I hate that Abby and the rest of them are even *here*, asking rude questions and hogging my mirror and turning my calm, quiet haven of a bedroom into chaos. I hate that getting ready alone with me apparently isn't enough for Syd anymore, that she doesn't realize how much I need her—and *only* her—right now.

"I have to do my makeup," I say, and then I hurry down the hall and lock myself in the bathroom before anyone can object.

Not that they would, probably.

I open the medicine cabinet and grab the tube of mascara my aunt once left here, but I have almost no practice putting it on, and I'm shaky with anger and nerves, which makes it even harder. I poke myself in the eye three times before I give up and throw the stupid mascara brush into the garbage as hard as I can. What does it even matter if my eyelashes look "supersize" and "clump-free," as the tube promises, when I'm probably about to crash and burn in front of hundreds of people?

The waking nightmare that's been haunting me for weeks pops into my head before I can stop it. *There I am in the center of the stage, spotlight shining down on me, countless eyes and camera lenses staring straight at me. Tess counts us off, and Faith launches into the bass riff of "Hear Us Roar." I grip the microphone tight in my sweaty fingers. I've practiced this song a million times; I can practically sing it in my sleep. But the bright lights are disorienting, and that familiar panic starts creeping up my throat, and when I open my mouth to sing, all that comes out is a horrifying, raspy croak.*

I grip the sides of the sink and gasp for breath. I can't be the lead singer of a band. Joining Heart Grenade was supposed to be a small, comfortable step on the way to something scary, and now it's gotten completely out of control. If I freaked out at a choir concert, it would be pretty bad, but if I screw up in front of the TV cameras tonight, it'll be so much worse. *Everyone* will see—my parents, my grandma, my choir director, thousands of strangers I don't even know. By this time tomorrow, the entire town could be laughing at me.

I should probably just stay here in the bathroom until the broadcast is over. It's not like anyone can force me to go. Maybe if I text Carmen again and I tell her I can't handle the pressure, she can get a ride home from the wedding in time to—

There's a knock on the door. "Gen?" calls Syd's voice.

"Yeah?" My voice comes out shaky.

"Can I come in?"

I'm not totally sure if I want her to, but I turn the lock and say, "Okay."

She slips inside and closes the door. She's wearing her dress now; it's the same light blue as her eyes, and tiny sparkles glint along the neckline. Her hair is pinned up in a simple twist.

"You look pretty," I say.

"Thanks! So do you. There's one thing missing, though."

"I tried to put on makeup, but I don't think I—"

"Not that. This." Syd opens her hand, and there in the center of her palm is the silver music-note necklace her grandma gave her after her violin recital last year. She wears it almost every day.

"That's your favorite, though," I say.

"It's just a loan. I thought maybe you could wear it for good luck, if you want." She smiles, and the dimple in her left cheek peeks out at me.

I smile back. "Yeah, okay. Thanks." If she's giving *me* her favorite necklace, maybe that means I'm still more important to her than her other friends.

I hold my braid out of the way while she clasps the chain around my neck. "It looks good," she says.

I glance at my reflection, and it *does* look good. I feel a little more confident with the music note nestled between my collarbones, but only a little.

"You ready for tonight?" Syd asks.

I waver for a second about whether to tell her the truth. But when I meet her eyes in the mirror, she looks like the best friend I've had since I was seven, and for a minute it's possible to forget about how my bedroom is full of newer, shinier people. "I don't think I can do this," I say. "I'm supernervous. Like, so, *so* nervous."

"Of course you're nervous. You're going to be on TV. It's incredibly scary. But it's also *really* exciting, and you're a great singer, and I know you're going to rock everyone's faces off."

Bizarrely enough, hearing that I *should* be scared makes me feel better. When it comes down to it, Syd always knows the right thing to say. "You think?" I ask.

"Definitely. And I'll be there in the front row, cheering you on. Keep your eyes on me and pretend nobody else is there, okay? You can totally do this."

"Okay," I say. And for the briefest moment, alone in the bathroom with my best friend, I feel like maybe I can.

ELLIE { **6:48 P.M.** }

THERE'S NO MIRROR IN MY ROOM, BUT IT doesn't matter. I can feel how absolutely perfect this dress is. I twirl until I'm dizzy, the petticoat underneath brushing against my legs.

I picture dancing with Kevin. My first dance with a boy. The DJ will play a slow song, and Kevin will spin me in circles. He'll be wearing a perfectly pressed suit, and I'll be wearing the rose corsage he brought me, pinned to my dress.

I pull my journal out of my sock drawer, flop down into my desk chair, and frantically scribble my thoughts and feelings. I want to hold on to this moment so I can write about it later.

Maybe it will be a love poem—my first real one—or perhaps I'll turn my experience tonight into a short story. I've never written a romance before.

My thoughts are interrupted by a soft knock on the door, and my chair falls over when I stand up too quickly.

"Come in," I say as I pick up the chair and slide it underneath my desk.

My soon-to-be stepmom, Soo-jin, slowly cracks the door open and peeks her head inside. When she sees me, her hand flies up to her mouth.

"Oh, Ellie." She drops her hand and sighs. "I can see why you told me you didn't need to go dress shopping. You look beautiful."

"Thank you." I look down at my dress, smoothing the skirt as I do. "It's the first time I've ever worn this."

"Well, it's magnificent." Soo-jin walks all the way into my bedroom and shuts the door behind her.

"It was my mom's." I blurt it out before thinking. Once I realize what I said, I cringe.

"Oh, Ellie." Soo-jin steps closer to me with her arms out, like she wants to give me a huge hug, but she stops short. Instead, she takes one of my hands in hers. "Don't ever feel like you can't talk about your mother. I know she was a special lady."

I give her a weak smile. My mom was more than a special lady. She was my best friend—truth be told, my *only* friend. My heart hurts as I think of how much I miss her, and I swallow the lump that's growing in my throat. "She loved Jane Austen."

Soo-jin nods. "This dress looks just like something Jane Austen would have worn to the ball."

I smile, a great big one this time. "That's exactly what I was going for." I pull the elbow-length white gloves from my dresser and slip them on. "This completes the look, I think."

Soo-jin's eyes widen, and she gives a little squeal. "I'll be right back," she whispers. She throws open my bedroom door and flies down the hall toward the room she shares with my dad. After a few seconds, she runs back to me, something glistening in her hands.

"What is that?" I ask.

"Close your eyes."

And even though my eyes are shut, I can see her beaming face in my mind. I feel something land on the top of my head, and before I can even imagine what it is, Soo-jin tells me to open my eyes.

Soo-jin takes a step back and looks at me like she's never seen me before. "Now it's perfect."

My hands flutter up to my head, and I feel the band in my hair.

"Come with me." Soo-jin gives a little nod and leads me to her room. She flicks the light on, steers me to the full-length mirror in the corner, and I am face-to-face with myself.

Sort of.

I mean, I know it's me. Of course it's me.

But I'm . . .

I'm *pretty*.

Soo-jin has put a pearl-covered headband in my hair. The jewels match the buttons on my dress perfectly. It's just the look I was going for, and I feel like I stepped right out of *Pride and Prejudice*.

My mother would have approved.

"Thank you, Soo-jin." I hug her ever-so-lightly so I don't wrinkle my dress. "It's beautiful."

"It is." Soo-jin smoothes my hair. "It belonged to my mother, and I know you'll wear it well."

"I will." I take a deep breath.

"Are you nervous?" Soo-jin asks. I look back at the mirror to see if anxiety is written all over my face. But the only thing I see is a pimple that's been there since Tuesday.

I nod. "I mean, it's my first dance."

Soo-jin gives me a knowing grin.

"But I'm glad it's with Kevin."

"Well, he's a very lucky boy," Soo-jin says.

I turn from the mirror and look at her. "I'm the lucky one. Kevin Wilton is the most handsome boy at school. I still can't believe he asked me."

"Of course he asked you, Ellie! You're a wonderful girl."

"It's just that . . . he's probably the most popular boy in our class. He could go to the dance with anyone, but he asked *me*. He realized he'd like to spend the evening with someone he can talk to, someone he can have an intelligent conversation with."

I keep going. I don't usually share this much, but there's something about Soo-jin that makes me go on and on. Since my mother died five years ago, there's been nobody I could talk to—besides my journals, that is. Until she came along.

"We were in the library. I was working on my novel—the one about the time-traveling princess—and was so into it that I didn't see him coming. He coughed to get my attention, and you could imagine how shocked I was to see Kevin Wilton— *the* Kevin Wilton—standing there. He asked if he could see my algebra homework. At first I thought he was going to copy my answers, and my heart sank a little. He's quite smart, and I know he could do it on his own if he tried. But all he did was look at my paper for about two seconds, and then he pulled out the chair next to mine."

"And then?" Soo-jin looks at me like I'm about to read off the winning lottery numbers.

"He sat in the chair, backward. He always sits in chairs backward. And then he looked right in my eyes and asked me if I would go to the dance with him."

"That's very romantic."

"It was." I sigh. "Just like in my daydreams."

I've been in love with Kevin since first grade, ever since he told me he liked my poem about George Washington. It's not like we've talked much since, but I've always hoped he'd notice me again. And now he has.

"You deserve all the happiness, Ellie." For a second, Soo-jin looks like she might cry, but then her face brightens. "Can we go downstairs and take some pictures?"

I can't help glancing in the mirror one last time. I smile at the girl staring back at me.

I hold my skirt up as I carefully navigate the steps. The front door slams, and Ashlyn comes racing into the house. She's got a scowl on her face, which just gets more severe when she sees me.

"Ashlyn," Soo-jin says, "doesn't Ellie look beautiful?"

Ashlyn barely looks my way as she passes me on her way up the stairs. "She looks like a hundred-year-old doily," she mutters under her breath.

Soo-jin doesn't hear her, but I do. And I suspect that's just what Ashlyn had hoped for.

When my dad first told me about Soo-jin, the first thing he mentioned was that she had a daughter my age. I was thrilled. I had always wanted a sister, and this was the next-best thing. But then I found out that Soo-jin's daughter was Ashlyn, and my sisterly dreams burst into flames.

Of all the girls in the world, my new "sister" had to be Ashlyn. Ashlyn, who actually found *Little Women* boring. Ashlyn, whose idea of a good read is *Star* magazine. Ashlyn, who can't write anything that's longer than 140 characters.

At school, Ashlyn pretends she doesn't even know me. Of course, nobody would ever mistake us for sisters. And it's not because she's Korean and I'm white. It's because she's everything I'm not—outgoing, social, and gorgeous. While I eat lunch in the library alone, everyone wants to eat with Ashlyn.

While I'm invisible, everyone knows Ashlyn. While I don't have many friends, everyone loves Ashlyn.

And she reminds me of that every single day.

"Wait a minute." Ashlyn stops on the step above me. She's staring at my head, her face scrunched up like she's just been diving into dumpsters.

Soo-jin and I both stop and look up at her.

"Mom!" Ashlyn screeches. "Is that—is that Halmoni's pearl headband?"

"Yes, it is. And your grandmother would be so happy that it's being worn. Doesn't it match Ellie's dress perfectly?" Soo-jin touches the top of my head, tucking a piece of loose hair into the band.

"You always tell me I can't wear it because it's only for special occasions!"

"This is a special occasion, Ashlyn," Soo-jin begins. "And it matches Ellie's—"

"Whatever." Ashlyn turns around and stomps up the steps before Soo-jin can finish.

Soo-jin's lips form a thin line. "I'm sorry about her. She's just upset that . . . well . . . She's having a tough time adjusting to a blended family."

I want to tell Soo-jin that it isn't easy for me, either. Although my dad and Soo-jin have been together for a couple of years, we only moved in together a few months ago. It was really weird to go from living with just my dad to living with two more people, especially when one of them is Ashlyn. Our old, quiet life was replaced with blasting music and constant chatter (Ashlyn loves the sound of her own voice), but I still try to be kind.

Instead, I just smile. I don't want to upset Soo-jin; she's trying so hard to treat me like family.

While the doily comment still rings in my ears, I remind myself that Ashlyn isn't going to the dance. At least I don't have to wonder if she'll make snarky comments about me in front of her friends. Without Ashlyn there, I can focus on someone who sees my good traits. I can focus on Kevin.

Soo-jin positions me in front of the fireplace. Then she calls my dad out of his office. Dad refuses to learn how to use a smartphone, so Soo-jin hands him the camera while she fusses with my dress.

Dad pauses before he snaps the picture.

"Oh, sweetie. Your mother's dress looks beautiful on you." Dad smiles, but it's one of those sad smiles where his mouth looks happy but his eyes look faraway. "She would be so proud right now."

I smooth the bodice of my dress and nod. I'm afraid if I try to say anything, I'll start to cry. And I don't want to have puffy eyes and a blotchy face when Kevin sees me.

Soo-jin touches my father's arm. He gives her a warm grin, shakes his head a bit, and then points the camera in my direction.

"Ready?" He adjusts the lens as I contemplate how to stand. Hands at my side? Hands on my hips? I have no idea where my hands are supposed to go.

I decide to leave them at my sides, and my dad snaps away, with Soo-jin beaming behind him.

"Look at the time," Soo-jin says as she glances at Dad's grandfather clock hanging on the wall. "Are you ready to go?"

"What about the young man who'll be taking you? Isn't he coming to pick you up?" Dad asks.

"We're meeting in front of the school," I say. "He's getting a ride."

Dad frowns. "That's not very gentlemanlike."

Soo-jin laughs. "That's the way kids do things these days."

Dad shakes his head, but Soo-jin has a way of lightening

the mood. "It will be fine, Ed. Ellie will have a wonderful time."

"I'm sure she will." My dad gives me a kiss on the cheek.

"Ashlyn!" Soo-jin calls up the stairs. "Let's go. You have to be at the Terzettis' in twenty minutes."

"Okay, okay." Ashlyn sounds more annoyed than usual. "I'm coming."

My heart speeds up as Soo-jin pulls her car keys off of the hook near the front door.

This is it.

I contemplate throwing my journal into my handbag but decide against it. Tonight, I'm going to live life instead of only writing about it. I take a deep breath and begin the best night ever.

ASHLYN { 7:02 P.M. }

"I DON'T SEE WHY I HAVE TO BE STUCK babysitting while *she* gets to go to the dance."

"In English, Ashlyn!" Mom says, jerking her head toward our minivan's backseat, where Ellie is fussing over that medieval-looking dress she's wearing. Ugh.

Ugh on the dress. Ugh on Ellie. Ugh on the fact that Mom and I can't talk in Korean unless we're all alone, because she doesn't want the new Love of Her Life (I like the guy, but still . . . puke!) or my weird stepsister-to-be to feel left out. Ugh on this whole miserable night.

Ellie is totally quiet when we pull up to the school, but I

can practically feel her bouncing back there. It only annoys me more to know she's so excited. I slouch waaaaaaaaay down in my seat, pretending to text on my phone, but really I'm trying not to get spotted by anyone I know. My closest friends are all very much aware that I'm grounded, of course, because I've been texting up a storm all day. But I can't help feeling like I'm letting the rest of the seventh grade down by not being there to show off any awesomeness at the dance tonight, especially since it's our first school dance and especially ESPECIALLY after all the hints I dropped about the new look I'd planned to debut. It's so unfair.

My mother is still being extra nice to Ellie. I guess it wasn't enough to give her *my* grandmother's headband. Now Mom's fawning all over her and offering to help her out of the car so her dress doesn't get caught in the door. I don't get why my mother can't see how perfectly embarrassing Ellie is. She's so . . . *awkward*. And smart, but not in a cool way *at all*. She's your basic year-one Hermione Granger.

But Mom acts like she's captivated by everything that comes out of Ellie's mouth. She's *never* listened to me discuss the pros and cons of the Pantone Color Institute's designated color of the season (peacock blue, for the record) with half the attention she gives Ellie when *she* blathers on and on about books written a gazillion and ten years ago. Who even knows— or cares!—what a green gable is? And why is my mother so overly interested in Ellie anyway? It's not like she's her *real* daughter. Shouldn't I come first?

"Thanks, Soo-jin," Ellie says in her soft, meek voice. At least she's not calling her "Mom" like my mother actually suggested last week. I . . . would not be cool with that. At all.

"Have fun," I mutter as Ellie exits, because otherwise I'll never hear the end of it from Mom, who waves at Ellie on the curb for literally an entire eon before finally pulling away. Why Ellie insists on waiting for Kevin outside instead of going in and getting warm is beyond me. Probably some romantic date scenario she has in her head of him showing up in a horse-drawn carriage or something. The girl is loco.

I slide up in my seat once we're on the move. "Seriously, I don't get why I have to take Ellie's babysitting job tonight while she has all the fun!"

"Would you like me to list the reasons, Seo-yeon?" my mom replies. Her voice is all calm and deadly, *and* she uses my Korean name instead of the American one I chose for myself when I started school. She only does that when she's genuinely mad. She doesn't even wait for me to answer before she starts in. "Number one: Because you thought it would be appropriate to post a photo to Instagram of your sister sleeping with topical treatments on her face, earning you the much-deserved grounding. Number two: Because Ellie is a very responsible girl and felt bad about canceling on her regular Saturday-night babysitting job. Do you know she was prepared to skip the dance when she found out Mrs. Terzetti hadn't been able to find a replacement? *That* didn't seem at all fair. The girl's been walking on clouds ever since Kevin asked her to go with him."

Well.

I have my own list:

Ellie is *not* my sister, and she won't be after the wedding either, no matter what Mom wants to tell herself. I was very fine being an only child and having my mother's undivided attention, thankyouverymuch.

Let's call a spade a spade, as my history teacher, Mr. Feldman, would say. Topical treatments = zit cream. Zit. Cream. And in my personal opinion, Ellie should use even more of it.

I don't think it's fair that *I* get stuck with bratty kids just because *Ellie* got asked to the dance. Which I am having serious trouble believing anyway. If she weren't too goody-goody to lie, I would totally suspect her of making the whole Kevin thing up. I mean, I know Kevin pretty well, and "Kevin + Ellie" does not compute.

It's all just soooooo maddening. This night is *the worst*.

I ring the doorbell, and Mrs. Terzetti answers right away. "Hello there—come on in. You must be Ashlyn. Ellie has *such* nice things to say about you!"

She does? Eww. Why?

I shrug out of my coat and hand it to Mrs. Terzetti, who says, "The girls are in the kitchen, making s'mores in our microwave. I'm afraid they're a smidge disappointed about not getting Ellie tonight, but I have no doubt you'll win them right over."

Smiling through closed lips, I walk in the direction she indicates, while behind me Mrs. Terzetti calls, "Girls, she's here!"

I'm here. Yippee.

The twins have their backs to the kitchen door, and their matching leggings-clad butts face me as they kneel on stools at the island. When they spin around, their hands are completely covered in gooey Marshmallow Fluff and melted chocolate.

The act of turning so fast makes one of the chairs all wobbly, and the girl on the left shrieks and grabs for me as it gives out under her. All I can focus on are globs of stickiness headed straight for my hair, and I jump back as quickly as I can. That was close!

The girl falls to the floor alongside the clattering stool. Whoops.

But I stand by my choices. Not even the $27-a-bottle L'Italy conditioner I got for my thirteenth birthday (the very same kind *Teen Vogue* model Allandra Esposio uses, I'm just saying) would help with Hair de S'more.

Mrs. Terzetti comes in just then, and she immediately picks her daughter up and wraps her arms around her. "Hope, baby, what happened? Are you okay?"

Hope Baby glares at me. "I want Ellie," she says, sticking out her tongue from over her mother's shoulder.

"Me too!" adds the other girl.

And I *want you to have Ellie. Trust me on that.*

"Hope, Charity, we've been over this. Ellie has special plans tonight, so she sent Ashlyn to hang out with you. Anyone cool enough for Ellie to be friends with is bound to be a great baby-sitter, right?"

Never have I ever heard the words "cool" and "Ellie" used in the same sentence. Wait until these girls get a little older and piece together that Ellie being available every single Saturday night except this one automatically rules out any possibility for coolness. I'm just saying.

Mrs. Terzetti releases Hope and crosses the room to dampen two paper towels before passing one to each kid. "Wipe your hands, girls. I've got to get going, and I want hugs good-bye that won't leave stains on my shirt." She glances down at her sweater. "Or any *more* stains, I should say."

Ugh. They'd better not even *think* of messing up my outfit. It's nothing fit for a dance, of course, but I'm rocking my yellow-and-white-striped slouchy shirt over dark-wash skinny jeans and tall boots. Especially with the white crepey scarf knotted oh-so-casually (okay, so it took me twenty minutes) around my neck.

She turns to me. "Mr. Terzetti had to work tonight, so I'm heading to the movies with some friends. I shouldn't be all that late. I wrote down our cell numbers on the pad on the fridge, and the girls know them too. They also know how everything runs around here, and they'll be happy to help you any way they can. *Right*, girls?"

The matching brats nod at their mother.

"Bedtime is eight thirty sharp because we have an early morning tomorrow. That means teeth brushed, stories read, lights out at eight thirty, not just beginning to head up to bed then, okay, girls?" Mrs. Terzetti waits for all three of us to nod, and then we follow her to the front hallway, where she gives her daughters even more hugs and kisses before finally closing the door behind her.

I pull out my phone and ask the girls, "Wi-Fi password, please?"

One of them rattles it off, and I wait for Instagram to load. As I do, I glance at the twins, staring gape-mouthed at me.

"What?" I ask.

"Ellie always plays with us the *whole* time," one says.

I raise my eyebrows and smile sweetly. "The thing is, girls, I'm not Ellie. I'm as far from Ellie as it's possible to get."

They narrow their eyes at me, so I try again. Geez, what's so hard about this? "You two won't know anything about this kind of important grown-up stuff because you're only, what, seven?"

Both of them put their hands on their hips. "We're EIGHT AND THREE-QUARTERS!"

"Okaaaaaay. Anyway, there's a dance tonight that's a

superbig deal, and I'm not *there* because I'm stuck *here*, but that doesn't mean I can't monitor every second of it on Instagram. So I'm probably gonna be pretty busy. Which means it would be great if you guys could find something to do to entertain yourselves."

Hope and Charity look at each other, and Hope's eyes grow big. "You mean you're not going to be paying *any* attention to us?"

Oooh! App loaded! Omigosh, Mariah's photo of herself in the green face mask. Hilarious! There's another picture of her trying on her dress, and I'm 99 percent sure it's the exact same one Tess was wearing in the picture *she* put up an hour ago. Holy cow. Those two hate each other. This is gonna be major drama! I need to find Tess's post in my feed to confirm.

Charity (or maybe it's Hope, who can tell?) clears her throat. "Did you hear us?" she asks.

"Hmm? What? Oh yeah, sure, whatever. Go crazy. Just don't burn the house down."

Okay, now *where* is that Tess picture?

RYAN { 7:17 P.M. }

STREAMERS TEAR EASILY. IF THERE'S ONE thing I'm going to take away from tonight, it's that. I've made a third rip in a red one I'm hanging when Mariah catches me.

"I know we're running crazy behind schedule, but please be careful about tearing those!" she says. "We only have a few rolls, and the gym has to look over-the-top fantastic tonight!"

From my spot on the ladder, I look out over the gym ceiling, which has a billion and one beams. There is no way a few rolls of streamers are going to cover all of that.

Mariah is standing at the bottom of the ladder, staring

down at her clipboard. She's supposed to be helping me, but she seems to have moved on to whatever the next item on her to-do list is.

Right now what I need is tape. Tape will fix the torn streamers. I slowly move down the ladder's rungs. When I signed up for the dance committee, nobody mentioned I'd have to risk my life on the tallest ladder in the universe. Of course, I only signed up for the dance committee in order to spend more time with Mariah. I thought that maybe, *possibly*, it would get me out of the friend zone I seem to be permanently stuck in with her.

I'm halfway down the ladder when a sudden light blinds me. *Someone really* is *trying to kill me*, I think, pausing until I can see again. When the bright, flashy things do finally fade, I look over to see a guy holding a camera with a gigantic lens.

"For the yearbook," he says.

I've seen him in the hallway, but I don't know his name. He's one of the older kids—an eighth grader. Whoever he is, he needs to stop snapping pictures of people on ladders. Someone could fall!

Before I can tell him that, he takes off running, as if he's done something he wasn't supposed to. I look over at Mariah, who is staring after him. That's it. No more ladders—for a few minutes, anyway.

As if these decorations aren't enough to ruin my night, my mom is standing near the refreshments table, talking to one of my teachers. My mom is one of those eager-to-volunteer types who agree to do anything. Tonight that means she'll be chaperoning the dance. I'm just hoping nobody figures out who she is.

I'm praying she won't let anything slip about my crush on Mariah. I try not to talk to my mom about it, but for a couple of years now she's annoyed me with comments about "my little friend," using a knowing mom tone that makes me cringe. Yep, moms seem to just guess these things.

"Where are you going?" Mariah asks, glancing at the empty ladder as I step onto firm ground. I wince. She *would* choose now to start paying attention to me.

"I need clear tape," I say. "Streamer repair."

Mariah squints at the ceiling, probably noticing that my streamer work is far from done. I figure there's some Scotch tape in the school office. If not, we'll be in trouble.

"Mariah," I say, standing directly in front of her. "Chill."

I know it sounds crazy—telling someone to chill out about streamers—but that's exactly what it takes to calm her down.

She takes a deep breath, and right in front of me she seems to go from a big ball of stress to the happy-but-in-charge Mariah I've always known.

Without warning, Mariah yells, "Chris!" at the top of her lungs. Chris is one of the committee members; actually, he's the only other guy on the committee besides me. They always have a hard time tracking down guys to help out, except for me, the guy who signed up because he has a crush.

Chris appears from out of nowhere. Mariah grabs the streamers from my hand and holds them out to Chris before pointing at the ladder. "Could you help us out and finish the streamers, please? We're going to get tape."

And that is how I end up walking to the school office with my best friend–slash–major crush less than twenty minutes before the dance is supposed to start. I have no doubt Chris can get the streamers hung, especially since I saw some girl come running over to help while we were walking out, but as head of the dance committee, surely Mariah has better things to do than go to the office with me. Could this maybe, *possibly*, mean she's starting to *like* like me? A guy can hope.

"Would you help me?" Mariah says as we walk, looking at me with big, sad, pleading eyes. "Leif's going to be here soon, and I have to make myself look awesome before he arrives. Can you cover for me with the decorations?"

"Leif?" I ask, swallowing around the big lump in my throat.

"Yes. Leif. My date." She avoids my eyes.

Okay, that lump is even bigger now. Since when is Mariah interested in Leif? Actually, it's not a huge surprise that she didn't tell me. For some reason, she never talks to me about crushes and stuff.

There's also the fact that I spent half of first period yesterday listening to Tess talk about how excited she is that Leif is taking *her* to the dance.

"Wait a second," I blurt as we round the corner to the office. "Leif is your date?"

When Mariah looks at me, she's frowning. I instantly realize that my words came out wrong. She thinks I'm saying she isn't pretty enough to go out with the guy all the girls want.

"I mean, it's just—" I start to say.

"What?" she interrupts.

I look over and see the worry in her eyes, and with a sinking feeling realize that *I* put that worry there. Mariah may be an "overachiever," as my mom calls her, but she's also one of the most sensitive people I've ever known. She cried for an hour and a half when she didn't make it into Heart Grenade.

No way can I tell her that Tess thinks he's *her* date. But I don't want her to be upset, and I especially don't want to be the person to make her cry. She'll find out about Tess eventually.

See, Tess is Mariah's biggest rival. The two of them have competed in almost every contest since second grade, when Mariah won the spelling bee and Tess stomped off.

So I snap my mouth shut, then shake my head. *Move along, nothing to see here.*

"Anyway," Mariah says, "wait until I change into my dress. It's going to totally wow him. My mom thought it was so adorbs that I had my first dance date, she let me buy something brand-new."

The sucky thing about having a girl best friend is that she talks about things like clothes and hair and makeup sometimes—stuff that I couldn't care less about. Mariah isn't like that usually, though. When she starts going on and on about girly stuff, I just focus on how cool she is. Not only does she have a soft, round face and dark shoulder-length hair that perfectly matches her big brown eyes, she's also the nicest and funniest and best person I know. She has an amazing personality, and her smile can light up a room. Not to mention, she has the biggest heart. She'll spend most of tonight trying to make sure everyone has a good time . . . when she isn't making googly eyes over her date, that is.

"So I said, 'Do you have a date for the dance?' and he shrugged like this." Mariah shrugs, but she has a huge smile on her face, which I doubt is a good impersonation of Leif, since he rarely wears an actual expression. "And I said, 'Do you want to go with me?' and guess what he said?"

"Yes?" I ask. The obvious answer because she's already said he's her date tonight.

"Nope. He said, 'Whatever,'" she corrects me proudly.

I throw her a confused look.

"'Whatever,'" she repeats. "That was his answer. Isn't that the cutest?"

I'm not sure how long I stand there, staring at her, before finally speaking. "Yeah. The cutest."

My words are meant sarcastically, but she doesn't even seem to notice. She's never opened up to me about crushes before, so why now?

Not that I've been all that open with Mariah, even though I've had a crush on her since we started middle school last year.

Before that, I just thought of her as my best friend. We met in second grade, when she moved into the house next to mine. My family relocated across town a few years later, but luckily I didn't have to change schools, so our friendship stuck. I've been scared to tell her I like her, though, for obvious reasons. Namely that she'll be all weird and our friendship will cease to exist.

Besides, if she *did* like me, she wouldn't have agreed to go to the dance with Leif. (Even though I'd been too chicken to ask her.) She certainly wouldn't be talking to me about him now.

I should have just worked up the courage to ask her to the dance.

These thoughts roll through my head as we arrive at the school office, which is empty. It's sort of creepy. I've only been in here a couple of times, but it's always full of activity: teachers running around, phones ringing, printers spitting out pieces of paper. Now it's just . . . quiet.

"The tape's back here somewhere," Mariah says, heading straight for one of the desks. Mariah helps out in the office after school sometimes, so she knows her way around.

While I'm waiting for her, I have even more time to think. Mariah and Leif. Leif and Tess. I'm pretty sure Leif doesn't really care that much about girls. Most of my guy friends don't. They're into sports and hanging out and getting through the school week so they can shoot hoops or play video games on weekends.

And now that I know Mariah likes Leif, I want to stop liking her. I just don't know how to do it.

As Mariah heads back toward me, tape in hand, the door opens behind me. It hits me in the butt, actually. I spin around to find Claudia from Heart Grenade standing there, her face all red.

"Have you seen Tess?" she blurts. She sounds out of breath, like she's been running.

"Nope," I say. And I hope, hope, hope she doesn't mention anything about Leif. Ugh.

I probably should *want* Claudia to say something about Tess and Leif; then Mariah will know he's a jerk for lining up two dates to one dance. But if she finds out that Leif asked someone else, she'll probably be hurt, and I don't want to see that.

Unfortunately, she's going to find out for herself soon enough . . . probably about ten seconds after Leif arrives. And then maybe she'll cry on my shoulder.

"Tell Tess I'm looking for her when you see her," Claudia

says. Then she takes off. I swear, she's running so fast, she's probably halfway down the hall before the door finally shuts behind her.

"Uh . . . no," Mariah says from behind me. I jump. I didn't even hear the door between the waiting area and the behind-the-desk area swing open and closed! She hands me the tape, speeds around me, and heads to the door.

"No what?" I ask, trying to match her pace. Mariah is speed-walking down the hall, and even with my long legs, I have to almost run to keep up with her.

"No, I won't tell her anything," Mariah says. "I don't talk to Tess. Ever."

There it is. The same old rivalry, heating up *again*.

"Especially after she took my spot in Heart Grenade!" Mariah continues. I can hear that tremble in her voice that I know means she's really, really mad.

I swear, her steps are getting angry now too. *Stomp. Stomp. Stomp.*

"I practiced all summer for that drummer spot," she seethes. "Plus, I had a play drum set that I loved when I was a kid, remember? I was obviously destined to be a drummer! I totally would have rocked it on that stage!"

I have to keep my mouth shut because Tess is a *real* drummer. It's what she does. Mariah's brother has a drum set in their basement, so Mariah decided to learn how to play over the summer. She didn't do it *only* to beat Tess for the spot in Heart Grenade, but when the opportunity arose to audition, she took it. Except the auditions took place at the beginning of the school year, about a billion days ago at this point. She should be over it.

I can't say that to her, though. All I can do is support her by agreeing that Tess is evil. That's what being a good friend means. Right?

"You're an *awesome* drummer," I say as I rush to keep up with her. "Heart Grenade would be so much better with you. Someday they'll realize that."

Mariah comes to a complete stop in the hallway, going from sixty to zero in a heartbeat. Luckily I'm a few steps behind, so I have time to slow down without zooming past her.

"Thanks," Mariah says.

She's looking at me with this sweet, sappy expression on her face. She used to get that look all the time, though lately it seems as if she hardly ever slows down to speak to me. Even when we hang out at my house or walk to our favorite taco place for lunch, she speeds through everything. She knows she does it; sometimes she even asks me to help her slow down. She says that no matter what she's doing in life, she feels like she has to always hurry to get to the next thing.

"Thanks?" I ask.

"You're a good friend," Mariah says. "You're my best friend. I don't know what I'd do without you."

That's when she hugs me. It's a friendship hug, not a boyfriend-girlfriend hug. She wouldn't hug Leif all quick and with her body far away like this. We don't really hug much anyway. Especially lately.

Even though we still hang out all the time, things have gotten awkward between us since middle school started. I can't really explain what it is, except that she sometimes stops talking right before she's about to say something. And there seems to be this awkward silence sometimes where she quickly averts her gaze when I'm looking at her. I like to tell myself it's because she likes me too, but I know that's just wishful thinking.

Okay, yeah, I'm not stupid. Mariah probably will never like me like *that*. Especially now that she likes Leif. If I could flip a switch and not like her anymore, I would. Maybe if I know I'll never, ever have a chance I can try to get over her. Until then, I'm cursed with thinking that everything she does is adorable.

"Now, let's get this dance going!" Mariah says, and she's off again, rushing down the hall while I race to keep up.

We round the corner and see the absolute last thing I want to see: Leif, looking all Leif-ish. He's just wearing pants and a sweater, but somehow he makes them look teen boy band–like. I want to puke.

"He-ey!" Mariah says, stretching the word into two syllables. I've never seen Mariah act all flirty and silly like this. It's weird.

"Hey," Leif says, not even coming close to cracking a smile.

I figure Mariah will stop to talk to him, but she just keeps going. She walks straight up to one of the faculty members who helped plan the dance and starts talking about music. That leaves me standing with Leif, feeling more than a little awkward. I have a cure for that, though.

"Gotta go," I say, planning a quick escape.

"Wait!" Leif says.

Uh-oh. This can't be good. I turn and walk back to him, because what else am I going to do? I notice him looking at Mariah with an anxious expression.

"Have you seen Tess?" Leif asks, shifting that anxious gaze toward the door to the school. It's still early, but a few students are already lingering in the hallway outside the gym doors.

"Nope," I say. "I don't think so. Someone was looking for her a few minutes ago."

He sighs. "Could you do me a favor?"

I know what he's angling for, and I want to say no. No, I'm not going to help him date two girls at once. Of all the guys at school, Leif is just too laid-back for me. No matter what you ask him, he just shrugs. It's like talking to a wall. I stand there and wait for him to say what that favor is.

"Could you keep Tess busy tonight?" he asks.

I'm surprised he asks me to keep an eye on *Tess*. He knows Mariah and I are friends; everyone does. Plus, I barely know Tess. Maybe he's so freaked out that he isn't thinking clearly.

"I'm pretty sure she'll be busy with the band," I point out.

"Yeah, but . . ." He looks around, then lowers his voice. "I kind of messed up."

"I know," I say, lowering my voice too. "What are you doing?"

"Man, I don't know," Leif whispers. "Tess asked if I wanted to go to the dance and I said, 'Whatever.' Then Mariah asked and . . . well, Mariah's kind of cute. I know she's your friend and all, so that's probably all kinds of cray to you."

Great. So he likes Mariah, not Tess. That's good for her, not so good for me. And I'm a really bad friend for it, but I can't quite be happy for her.

"Don't tell Mariah about Tess, man," Leif says. "You haven't already, right?"

"No."

"Cool." He thinks for a second, then says, "I just have to keep them apart, that's all. I need you to help keep them busy so they won't find out I'm here with both of them."

"I'll see what I can do," I say. Mostly I just don't want to see Mariah get hurt. But if keeping Tess busy gives Leif time to hang out with *my* crush, how can I get behind that?

"Sorry, I really need to get back to the gym," I say, moving away from him.

"See ya, man!" Leif calls as I head back toward the gym entrance. On the way, I see Mariah. She's somehow speed-changed into her dance outfit, and her dress is a total 180 from the jeans and T-shirt she was wearing earlier. I stare at her for a moment, noticing the way the dress brings out the highlights in her hair. Why does she have to be so amazing in every single way?

She looks at me and smiles; in that second, my heart does a little jumpity-jump, and I know I'll do anything she asks if she'll keep smiling at me like that.

As I head toward the gym, Mariah's face lights up and she marches straight to Leif.

Sighing, I head aimlessly in the opposite direction. I can't watch this. That's when I see Tess waiting outside, her back to the door. She already looks prepared to kick butt in those combat boots, and . . .

Wait.

At first I'm thinking that her dress looks familiar, but then I realize . . . it's the same dress Mariah is wearing! I come to a complete stop.

How am I going to keep Mariah from completely freaking out once she sees Tess has copied her dress *and* her date?

JADE { 7:28 P.M. }

I DO *NOT* WANT TO BE IN THIS LACQUER-floored cafe-gym-atorium. I don't even go to this school. But when you're totally robbed of a win in the biggest band contest in the whole city, you do what you have to do to make things right.

Uncle Garrett fiddles with the TV station's equipment, making sure all the cords are connected and that every lens is clean. He cleans the digital camera next, the one I'm in charge of, and hands it back to me.

"They want pictures for the station's social media, right? Is it okay if I go take some as kids come in?" I ask. I'm on photo duty for now, but for my plan to work I need access to the video camera before we go on the air. First things first, though; I have some recon to do, and the entrance is the perfect location to identify band members as they arrive.

"Sounds good, Jade," he says. "See if you can get some group shots too."

"On it," I say, heading for the doors. Red and gold streamers hang from the towering ceiling, which makes me wonder if I could have also planned some well-timed water balloon launches tonight. Oh well, can't think of everything.

When the teachers pull the gym doors open, it's like a noise tornado spins through the halls. And every sound echoes off the shiny floors and tile walls. I recognize a couple of the band members from the totally rigged Battle of the Bands (one of their aunts *and* a family friend were on the committee—SO not fair), but everyone else blends into the Lynnfield Middle crowd. All the colorful pastel dresses whip by me in a blur as I search for Carmen, Heart Grenade's lead singer. But I don't see her anywhere. A girl in a leopard-print skirt and a pair of Chucks walks by me; for some reason she looks terrified, but I love her for not caving in to the expected semiformal wear like everyone else.

I snap some pictures to do the job I'm here for and to make sure my cover isn't blown. It took a whole lot of convincing to get Uncle Garrett to agree to let me help him with tonight's show. Something about the station's insurance coverage and very, very expensive equipment. After two deliveries of chocolate chip cookies (his favorite) and a promise to go shopping for craft supplies with my cousins (like they're always begging me to do), he finally gave in. It'll all be worth it to make things right.

I manage to get kids to stop and pose for pictures by telling them I'm the photographer for the station. People will do anything when they think they'll be on TV. Some groups squeeze in and wrap their arms around one another with big, happy smiles on their faces, while others insist on doing bunny ears, sticking out their tongues, and doing that disgusting eyelid-flip thing. And plenty of kids walk right by me, talking nonstop about how they can't wait to see the band play.

If they get to play, I think to myself.

I'm pretty sure someone mentions adding something teeth-staining to the punch too, and while I have no intention of reporting them, I do take a quick picture of the possibly guilty group of kids just in case. Plus, dealing with a silly gag might provide a nice distraction for the chaperones while I get things done.

Now to find my accomplice. He goes to Lynnfield, but he's agreed to help me, and I need to make sure we're all set with what has to be done. Unlike my uncle, my accomplice took no convincing at all. All I have to do is put in a good word for him with Uncle Garrett for the summer internship at the TV station. I send a check-in text.

Hey. It's Jade. Is everything in place?

No response. Well, I can't stand here waiting for him to answer. I've got a job to do.

I head back into the gym and get back to the plan. "Hey, Uncle G, I was thinking that I'd be really great behind one of the video cameras tonight. You know I do it all the time at my AV club."

Uncle Garrett gives me a look. The kind that says *I need a minute to figure out how to politely tell you there's not a chance I'll say yes to that.* But I've prepared for this.

"Jade—"

"Wait, before you answer, just hear me out." I stand behind camera two, which has no one behind it to shoot close-ups for the show. "You guys are short-staffed because of Chocolate

Fest downtown, and as awesome as you are, there is no way one person can operate the close-up camera *and* the main one at the same time."

"Well, that was my plan," says Uncle Garrett. He looks over at the intern who's in charge of the sound feed tonight. He's sitting over in the corner of the gym with all the equipment he'll use to manage the sound during the band's performance. And I happen to know Uncle Garrett is more than a little nervous about not having more help for this event.

I try again. "If you tell me what close-ups you want, I'll get them for you. All I have to do is zoom in and zoom out. Zoom in, zoom out," I say again, pressing an imaginary button in the air to get my point across. "It's a no-brainer, really. Free labor and all."

Plus, I'll be able to focus the camera on whatever craziness happens onstage tonight.

But I'm not even sure my uncle is listening. He's too busy fiddling with wires and adjusting where the cameras are pointed.

He lets out a deep sigh.

"You're already flustered," I try again. "So let me help. Please?"

Uncle Garrett wipes the back of his hand across his

forehead. "It *would* be nice not to worry about two camera feeds," he says. "Let me double-check to see if the station is sending anyone else over." He takes out his phone and heads to the corner where the intern is getting ready. I use the opportunity to check another little piece of the sabotage plan off the list.

I try to act like I'm happy to be here. I smile politely at random people as I get behind camera one, making sure I put myself right in the way of Uncle Garrett's view of the equipment. I don't want to make it malfunction—these things really do cost a fortune—but if I can make my *uncle* malfunction, well . . .

I take a little restaurant packet of pepper out of my pocket, tear it open, and sprinkle it on top of the camera. But it doesn't smell strong enough yet. I pull three more packets out and rip them all at once, checking over my shoulder to make sure I'm in the clear. Uncle Garrett is deep in conversation on his phone, so I'm good.

My nose starts to wiggle and I sniff at the smell, which grows stronger with every sprinkle. I can't help letting out a very loud *achoo*, getting the attention of a group of girls nearby. I put up my hand to let them know I'm fine, although it's not like anyone bothered to say *bless you*. Are they a bunch of Neanderthals at this school or what?

I stuff the empty packets back in my pocket. All set. My uncle can't have pepper in front of him on the dinner table without sneezing, let alone right near his face. Sorry, Unc, but I need this to work.

Finally I get a text reply.

Not exactly in place.

I step away from the pepper and write back.

What does that mean?!

I knew I should have smuggled in what we needed.

I'm working on it.

Great. What good is having an accomplice if he can't get the job done? Although it's not like I could have held interviews for the position.

The gym is slowly filling up, and all the padding on the walls doesn't seem to be helping to quiet the noise in the room. Girls are chatting, boys are laughing, there are even kids being all dramatic already, and the dance has barely gotten started.

"You sure you want to do this?" asks Uncle Garrett from behind me. I jump a little, the sound of his voice knocking me out of the careful observations in my head. I need to take in every detail for this to work.

I nod my head wildly. "Totally sure."

"Okay, but you'll be monitoring camera one, the stationary camera," he says.

Shoot. That means I peppered the wrong one.

"All you have to do is make sure it stays pointed exactly where it is and that no one bumps into it," he says. "I need you to follow instructions this time, understand?"

Okay, I might not have the best track record when it comes to proving I'm responsible (skipping out on babysitting my cousins and constantly forgetting to give Uncle G's messages to my dad come to mind), but I do know my way around video equipment. I hold back a sneeze from the pepper.

"Yes, I understand," I say. "I'll get the job done. Don't worry."

But he doesn't look away. He eyes me and smooshes his face up like he's reconsidering. I can't blame him; I probably wouldn't let me do it if I were him. I'm guessing he's thinking about last month, when I took the girls out for dinner, which consisted of ice cream and candy. Or maybe the time I offered to help with the garden and accidentally pulled out all the flowers instead of the weeds. (To be fair, they're superhard to tell apart sometimes.) It could also be that he still hasn't forgotten the Jade-snagged-an-early-piece-of-Aunt-Mariana's-birthday-cake incident.

He loves his job, and I admit, letting me help might not be the best career move for Uncle G. Plus, he's right; I'm actually *not* planning on following instructions very closely. He has every reason to worry.

"Jade, this is a big night for these kids, so I need you to stay focused," says Uncle Garrett.

"Oh, I'm focused for sure," I say. I'll admit, the guilt is slowly creeping its way through my body, trying to get me to change my mind. And okay, yeah, I do feel bad that my uncle will be caught in the middle of all this. But I can't back out now. I seriously can't. When our band was cheated out of that win, there were so many tears. We even had to do that thing where you put cucumber slices on your eyes to make them less puffy.

So I won't let anyone distract me from my mission tonight.

TESS { 7:33 P.M. }

TO SAY THAT I'M ANNOYED LEIF ISN'T here yet is probably the understatement of the year.

I told him to meet me in front of the gym next to the giant puffin statue at 7:20. If he thinks I'm going to wait out here by this ridiculous school mascot (since when are there puffins in Ohio, anyway?) when it's getting colder by the minute and my arms are covered in goose bumps, he's mistaken me for some other girl.

I mean, you'd think he'd be excited that I asked *him* to the dance. He didn't even have to do any work! He just had to get dressed and show up—on time. How hard is that?

I slide my phone into my boot. No way am I carrying a little purse. Because where would I put that when I'm onstage with the band? And these boots have plenty of room for anything I need to carry. I smooth my shimmery purple metallic dress and wish Mom had gone for letting me put a purple streak in my not-really-blond-but-not-really-brown hair to match it. That would've been killer. My best friend, Carmen, put red streaks in her hair last week and it looks crazy good. When we walked by together, everyone would've been like, "There go those two girls from that amazing band Heart Grenade. Did you hear they're going to be on TV?" Except Carmen's not going to be on TV, because her parents dragged her to a stupid wedding. I can't believe we're finally hitting the big time and she won't be here for it.

Carmen's parents are *way* more open-minded than my mom is (except when it involves skipping her cousin's wedding, apparently). When I asked Mom about putting streaks in my hair, she looked horrified and was all "No, Tess! Why would you ruin your beautiful hair like that?" So I went for the next-best thing and got these purple clip-in hair extensions at the mall. Mom liked those about as much as she liked me wearing my boots to the dance—meaning, not at all. Which is why I snuck them out in a bag that I've ditched behind the bushes outside the science lab. I put them in my hair using a compact that I stashed in my boot.

At least it's just me and Mom. I can't imagine trying to sneak past *two* parents with my not-exactly-traditional style. She'll find out what I'm wearing when I'm on TV with Heart Grenade tonight . . . but there are at least three hours until she picks me up and I have to deal with *that*.

My phone buzzes against my ankle as I'm rubbing my hands up and down my arms. I pull it out right as I spot that really quiet girl Ellie shivering on the sidewalk. She was here before I was, standing around like she's waiting for someone too. I wonder who she's going to the dance with. She's always seemed way more into books and daydreaming than guys. Her dress looks like something the women wear in those BBC movies Mom loves to cry over. It's different, that's for sure, but I'm the last person to judge different.

I check my phone. It's Carmen.

Sooooo bored. WHY am I here????

I promised I'd text Carmen updates all night. So I snap a picture of myself looking really ticked off (which I am) and send it to her.

L is late & this is how I feel abt it.

Seriously, if he couldn't get here by 7:20, why didn't he just *say* so?

"Heck no, we won't go!" This girl I don't recognize is marching down the sidewalk. She brushes past Ellie, holding a sign up above her head. Ellie sort of stumbles into the grass. If I were her, I would've pushed the girl right back, because really, how rude is that?

"If you agree, walk with me!" the girl shouts. I can't even read what's on her sign, and I'm kind of tempted to go over and ask her what she's protesting. I mean, if she's protesting the economy or whatever it is people protest about, there are probably way better places to do that than outside Lynnfield Middle. But I have bigger problems right now.

Like, where is my date?

Seven thirty-five. Whatever. He can meet me inside. I'm not standing out here and freezing any longer.

As I slide through the doors, I think—for just one second—about asking Ellie if she's coming in too. But she always has this terrified look on her face, like she wants to run away from me. So I don't ask.

In the lobby, music streams from the open gym doors

and kids are walking around all dressed up. It's weird to see people you go to school with wearing clothes way nicer than they normally do. Like, Ryan wouldn't be caught dead wearing that polo shirt–and–khakis getup to school. Ryan's eyes get big when he spots me, as if he's somehow surprised to see me here. I tilt my head, but he shuffles off through the lobby. Weird.

I head to the gym and bump past two boys who are taking up way too much space in the doorway.

"Hey!" one of them shouts when his drink sloshes over the edge of his cup.

I fix them with a glare. "Relocate." Then I smile. "Please. People need to get through here."

They slide off, muttering stuff I'm sure isn't very nice. But I don't really care. What I do care about tonight: 1) finding Leif, and 2) making sure my band doesn't implode onstage—and on TV!—without Carmen.

I move inside and spy Genevieve hovering near Sydney and a couple of other girls. Genevieve is supernew to the band *and* she's filling in for Carmen tonight. Carmen told me she thinks Genevieve is angling for her spot as lead singer, but I don't believe that for a second. Genevieve seems way too nice for devious plans, and I know that Carmen's just bummed that she can't be here tonight.

Genevieve looks a little freaked out as I approach her. I've barely had time to talk to her since she joined. I bet she's nervous about tonight. Her friends are laughing like crazy, but she's kind of quiet.

"Hey! You ready for the show?" I ask her.

She looks down and stubs the floor with the toe of one lime green Chuck. They're really cute. "Nice shoes," I add.

"They're too much, aren't they?" she asks.

"What? No. Of course not."

"Okay." She scans the crowd like she's looking for someone.

"Have you seen Leif?" I ask as I tap out a rhythm against my thighs with both hands. It's a habit I've had since I was a kid.

"Leif?" Genevieve asks. She's looking everywhere but right at me.

"Yessss . . . you know, blond hair, plays basketball, parents own the bank?"

I really don't care how much money Leif's family has or how good at basketball he is. I pegged him as the perfect guy to hang out at the dance with because he's smart. He was the only one who actually gave me any competition during the History Warriors competition last fall, and he was the only other kid from our school who got invited to the Greater Ohio Youth Leadership Conference. Not to mention that we check out the same books from the school library. So when he told me that my drum solo in Heart Grenade's "Hear Us Roar" was the best part of the song, and then gave me his yogurt in the cafeteria a few weeks ago when I forgot my lunch and had to make do with the freebie crackers and soy nut butter from the cafeteria, I decided he was the one I needed to ask. Not to mention that, well, he's cute. Like, really cute.

"Have you seen him?" I ask Genevieve again.

She shrugs. I'm going to take that as a no.

"Hey," she says. "I've been thinking about tonight. . . ."

"Yeah?" I'm listening while I scan the gym for Leif's white-blond hair, in case his brain backfired and he thought I said to meet him *inside* instead of outside. How anyone can actually have hair naturally that color is beyond me. He basically looks like he walked out of a Viking village and is going to pillage the art room or something (in a very cute way, of course).

"And I'm feeling—"

"There he is. Really. Do you think I could've been more clear that outside is *outside*, not in the gym? Sorry, but I need to catch up with him. I'll see you later." I stride into the mass of kids, eyes locked on Leif's shock of hair behind a big group of girls who are (for whatever reason) doing some kind of cha-cha line. I go right through them, and the two girls I push past jump away so fast you'd think I was a teacher coming to give them detention.

"Leif!" I shout over the music. At least fifteen people turn and stare at me. Hmm. Maybe I should dial it down a notch.

Except he didn't even hear me. And when I take a few more steps, I can see why. He's talking to the *one* person I'd be happy to never see again.

Mariah.

And she's wearing . . . I blink really hard, like that'll make everything change. It doesn't. When I open my eyes, she's still wearing a shimmery purple dress.

The *exact* same dress I have on.

My face goes hot, and my fingers are all twitchy when I yank my phone from my boot to text Carmen.

Mariah has my dress!!!!!! 😠 😠 😠

Are you serious??? Wish I were there. ☹

I wish she were too. I could use my best friend at my side right now. And I haven't seen Faith or Claudia, my other band-mates, here yet. Looks like I'm on my own.

I drop the phone into my boot, stretch out my fingers and curl them in, throw my shoulders back, and march right up to Mariah and Leif. "Mariah," I say in the iciest voice possible.

She tilts her head, and her eyes widen just a little when she sees my dress. "Tess," she says in an equally icy voice.

At that exact second, some kid flies up and blinds us with a camera flash. "Yearbook!" he shouts as he runs off. Good thing he's fast, because if he'd given me another second, his camera would be on the floor, in pieces.

"I didn't know you were coming. I thought you would've been home studying after that algebra test." I give her a smile. The whole school knows how annoyed Mariah was at the B she got on that test. She even spent ten minutes arguing with Ms. Huff about it after class. I got an A+, which she knows because Ms. Huff is one of those teachers who holds up the test with the highest grade and brags about the student who got it. It was the first time Mariah's test wasn't the one being shown off at the front of the room. My getting the top score was almost like payback for when she beat me for the Quiz Bowl captain's seat. Which was payback for my landing the gig as Heart Grenade's drummer last fall. Which was payback for her winning the school talent show in fifth grade. Which was payback for . . . yeah.

Mariah and I have a little history.

She tosses her shiny, shoulder-length dark hair like that B was nothing. But I know better.

"Nice dress," she says.

I make a noise that's not really a word. I'd never admit it, but a part of me wonders if she's wearing the dress better than me, with her simple heels and one-color hair.

I decide to ignore her. I found Leif, and that's who I was looking for anyway.

I angle myself so that Mariah's behind my back. "Hey, L, want to go grab something to drink?" I think he likes it when I call him L. At least, he hasn't said that he doesn't.

He shoves his hands into his pockets. His eyes dart between me and Mariah.

"Come on." I go to pull him away, but Mariah speaks up.

"Excuse me, Tess, but Leif and I were about to dance. Isn't that right, Leif?"

I drop my arm and spin around. "Okay, little problem with that. Because he's here with me."

Mariah blinks at me. "Um, no. He's here with *me*."

I laugh. She's probably mad that I asked him before she could. She doesn't even like him. She only wants to dance with him because she knows I asked him and she has this need to one-up me in everything.

"Right. Come on, L." I take a step away, but he doesn't follow.

Mariah's staring at him now. "Leif?"

Leif shrugs and looks off toward a group of his friends, who are bumping into one another and laughing.

Wait. What's going on here?

"Are you being serious?" I ask Mariah.

"Are *you*?" She's got her hands on her hips and looks madder than she was when I snagged the blue ribbon at the sixth-grade science fair over her second-place nutritional analysis project. I'd told her my homemade battery was going to take the whole thing, and I was right.

We both stare at Leif now.

He's looking everywhere but at us.

"Okay . . ." I turn my glare to Mariah. "I thought you'd be

here with Ryan." They've been inseparable since third grade. And he's always gazing at her like she's the most important person in the world. In fact, I can see him watching us now from the doorway.

"Oh my God, no!" She actually flushes red. "He's my best friend. That would be so weird. I'm here with Leif. And besides, aren't you too busy with Heart Attack or whatever that band is to actually dance tonight?"

Puh-lease. She knows exactly what the band is called. She pretends to hate the music because she's jealous that I made it in and she didn't. It's probably eating her up that we won the contest and are going to be on TV.

"We don't go on till later. So no, I'm not too busy to dance. With Leif. Who is here with me, not you."

"With *me*, you mean," she says.

"I asked him on Monday." I raise my eyebrows. She's not going to win this.

"So did I."

"I asked him right after second period."

"I asked him at lunch."

"So technically, I asked first." I cross my arms and wait for her to admit defeat.

"Who cares? Obviously he changed his mind, because he told me yes!"

"Then why don't we let *him* decide?" I swing around to hear him say that yes, of course he's here with me.

Except . . . he's gone.

I level a glare at Mariah. She pinches her lips together.

It is *so* on.

ELLIE { 7:38 P.M. }

I GOT HERE EXTRA EARLY SO I COULD have some time to calm my nerves before Kevin arrived, and now it's getting chilly. I wrap my arms around my waist to keep warm. A stream of cars pulls up to the front entrance, and kids make their way inside, laughing loudly and talking over one another.

I focus on each car door as it opens, waiting for Kevin to appear. I don't even know what his parents drive, but every time a car arrives, my stomach swirls and my heart speeds up.

A couple of girls from my Advanced Algebra class get out of a minivan. They see me and wave.

"Hi, Ellie." Amanda beams. "Your dress is so beautiful."

"Oh, thanks so much." I smile. "So is yours."

Amanda looks down and rolls her eyes. "It was my sister's from, like, ten years ago."

"Well, it looks really nice on you," I say. And I mean it. Amanda usually wears cardigans. Tonight, her sparkly emerald dress makes her whole face shine.

"You look great too, Lila." I touch her wrist. "I love how your bracelet matches your necklace."

"Thanks." Lila is so quiet I have to step closer to hear her. "I got the set for my birthday. Sapphire is my birthstone."

"Well, it suits you."

"Want to come inside with us?" Amanda shivers a little and wraps her shawl around her shoulders.

"Oh, I would." My face heats up. "But I'm waiting for someone."

I didn't tell anyone about Kevin, unless you count my journal, of course. I mean, sure, my family knew, but I didn't want to share it with anyone at school. Partly, I didn't want to sound like I was bragging. But mostly, I wanted to save it just for me, to keep it close, like a well-worn diary.

Amanda's eyes get huge, and she drops her voice to a loud whisper. "Do you have a date?"

"I guess I do." I look down at my shoes, trying to hide the smile that threatens.

"Oh, wow. That is so exciting. Who is it?" Amanda asks.

I figure it's okay to tell them now. They're going to see us dancing together soon enough, and then the story won't be mine alone anymore.

"Kevin asked me last week."

Amanda jumps up and down, and Lila lets out a tiny little squeal.

"Kevin is so cute," Amanda says, and Lila nods.

"And he's supernice," I add. "And smart."

Amanda crinkles her eyebrows, as if she doesn't quite believe me. I know Kevin doesn't do very well in school, but in my heart of hearts, I'm sure he has so much to offer. He likes to act like he's supercool, but I've seen him when he thinks nobody's looking—the focused look on his face when we have pop quizzes, the thoughtful way he browses for books in the library. No matter how cute he is, he has a lot of beauty on the inside as well.

"Brrrrr." Amanda shivers again. "It's getting chilly out here. We'll see you inside, okay?"

I nod, and Lila follows Amanda into the school. They're

nice, and we get along well in class, but we don't hang out at all. They live on the other side of town, and to be honest, they've never asked me. It's okay, though. My writing takes up so much of my free time, and I enjoy spending my weekends babysitting. I mean, sure, it would be nice to be friends with someone my own age, but at least when I play Scrabble with the twins, I know I'm going to win!

Another car pulls up, and two boys I don't recognize get out. I pluck my antique pocket watch out of my beaded clutch—the watch belonged to my mother's father before she gave it to me—and check the time. It's seven forty. I'm sure Kevin said he'd meet me outside at seven fifteen. At the statue, he'd said. I slide the watch back into my bag and scan the next car that pulls up.

No Kevin.

As I glance at the headlights lining up at the curb, one voice overpowers the collective voices of students streaming into the school. The girl who nearly knocked me over earlier, some sort of protester, is walking my way—running, almost—carrying a sign over her head. I jump out of her way as I squint to try to make out the words. I can't tell what it says, but she's yelling, "Heck no, we won't go!" I wonder what she's protesting about. Women's rights? Or maybe school lunches.

A car door slams behind me, and a boy laughs. I turn quickly to see if it's Kevin, but I can't tell from where I'm standing, so I take a few steps forward to get a better view. Just as the boy steps out, I stumble on a crack in the sidewalk.

I squeeze my eyes shut, praying that the boy getting out of the car isn't Kevin. I would hate for him to see me being so clumsy.

I straighten up and slowly open one eye, then the other. I don't recognize the passenger, and in fact, he barely looks at me.

I wonder where Kevin can be.

Maybe he's late because he's nervous. Maybe he's pressing his suit so it will look just right. Maybe he's having trouble with his tie. Or maybe it's not his fault at all. What if his parents are having car trouble? And since I don't have a cell phone, he wouldn't even be able to let me know. I bite my lip. Maybe I should consider getting a phone. I sigh. Who am I kidding? Even if I wanted one, my dad wouldn't be on board. I know how much it bothers him that Ashlyn is always on hers, and he probably wouldn't think getting one so Kevin can reach me is a good enough reason.

The line of cars is getting shorter now. Still no sign of Kevin.

A couple of boys from my homeroom walk out of the school and onto the sidewalk.

"That was the lamest thing ever," one of them says to the other.

"Right? My ears still hurt from those girls singing along to that Beyoncé song at the top of their lungs." The other boy shakes his head.

"I'm never going to another dance again," the first boy says. "When is your mom going to be here?"

"I called her ten minutes ago to come get us, so she should be here soon."

"Cool. Let's just go to your house and play Minecraft."

"Excuse me." I walk over to the boys. "You've been inside?"

"Unfortunately," one of the boys says. "It's like a sauna in there."

"Did you by any chance notice if Kevin Wilton was inside?"

The boys look at each other, and one of them nods. "Yeah, I saw him."

Could it be that Kevin and I had a misunderstanding? I was so nervous as we made our plans. It occurs to me that if I was nervous, maybe Kevin was nervous too! A smile comes to my lips, and my gloved hand flies up to cover it.

That must be it. Kevin just forgot that we were supposed to meet outside. Or maybe he slipped in with a bunch of other kids and didn't notice me waiting. It did get pretty crowded out here.

"Thank you so much," I say to the boys, and then I lift my skirt a little and walk as fast as I can toward the door. I bite my lower lip, suddenly feeling awful that I've been making him wait all this time. He's probably looking everywhere for me. My stomach churns, and I'm nearly running now.

A wall of noise hits me as soon as I enter the building. A bunch of kids are walking around in the hallway, talking and shrieking and laughing. The band isn't on yet, but a DJ is playing music so loudly that I can actually feel it rumbling in my chest. I instinctively put my hands over my ears, but it doesn't help. Just before I get to the gym, I stop and lean against a wall. I close my eyes, take a deep breath, and picture Kevin. I see him smile as he asked me to come tonight. I picture him waiting patiently for me in the gym. I think about our first dance.

And then, right in the middle of wondering if Kevin is wearing a bow tie or a necktie, my mother's face pops into my mind.

Oh, how I wish she were here. She would kiss the top of my head, hold both of my hands, and tell me how happy she is for me. She'd tell me the story of her first dance, and her eyes would sparkle as she remembered the exact song that was playing. She'd take me to the cedar chest in her room, and we'd go through old pictures of her at my age. We'd giggle at her hairstyle and outdated clothes, and we'd marvel at how much I look like she did.

I squeeze my eyes shut. The image vanishes, but the hot tears that bubbled up linger for a few seconds. I take another deep breath, and amazingly, it helps me feel more calm. Somehow, just thinking of my mom fills my whole body with warmth. I don't know if I believe in heaven or the afterlife or any of that stuff, but I like to think my mom is somewhere not too far away, looking out for me.

With that thought, I smile, stand up as tall as I can, and head toward the music.

ASHLYN { 7:43 P.M. }

UM, HELLO? DARLING FRIENDS OF MINE?
WHY are you ignoring me? I relaunch my Instagram app in case
the Wi-Fi here at the Terzettis' is slower than Ellie trying to
catch on to one of my jokes. But no. When it refreshes, my
photo of the cute new suede boots I'm wearing for the first
time tonight (even though they really deserve an occasion and
not a babysitting gig for their debut) still has zero likes. Are
my friends all so seriously wrapped up in their precious dance
that they can't be there for me in my time of need? That is
just so—

"It kind of feels like you're ignoring us."

{ 90 }

Yes! That's exactly how I'm feeling! Oh, wait. That wasn't said *by* me . . . that was *to* me. I pick my head up and study the twin in front of me. Her brown hair is just past her shoulders and hangs limply, a perfect match to her sister's, as is her frumpy leggings-and-sweatshirt outfit. And her face, for that matter. It's almost creepy how identical they are. I hope they're not going to be offended that I literally have no clue who's who.

"Sorry, what?" I ask.

She tilts her head. "We were *wondering* if you're even going to play with us *at all* tonight?"

Um, no? My mother always jokes that she can't get me to do anything unless I'm "properly incentivized," but to be honest, I never understand why she laughs when she says it. Isn't that basically how our whole society works?

And at the moment, there are exactly zero reasons to be a model babysitter. I have no intention of ever doing this again.

Which means I don't need a glowing review from the Brats, as I've cleverly nicknamed them on my Instagram feed (as in *How did I get stuck watching the Brats while everyone else dances the night away?*).

The girl shifts her weight to her other foot, juts out a hip, and sighs deeply. "Are you just gonna stare at me, or are you going to answer my question?"

Weh-heh-*hel*. I dig the attitude. She might be going places, this one. I raise both eyebrows and level her with a look until she flinches and drops her eyes to the floor.

She might be going places, but I'm already there.

I examine my nails for chips in my gel polish (ugh—biggest pet peeve ever) while I consider her question. "What did you have in mind?" I ask.

I don't want to play anything with the Brats, but if Instagram is going to be all sad and lonely tonight, maybe doing something short with them could kill some time. The TV remote has approximately forty-seven thousand buttons, and I doubt these girls like me enough to explain any of them to me. I could always YouTube some instructions, but . . . let's just see what the Brats have in mind. Might not be terrible.

"We could play Monopoly," the one in front of me says, while her sister nods enthusiastically from the doorway.

Scratch that. It *could* be terrible.

I roll my eyes. "Waaay too confusing. I hate the whole mortgaging-properties thing. It makes zero sense, and plus, that game lasts, like, two lifetimes."

The other girl comes over. Side by side, the matchy-matchy thing they have going on is even more superannoying. Did they not get the memo: No one does you better than *you*! Why risk any evidence to the contrary standing off to your right?

Hmm. I wonder . . .

I squint a bit and study them. "I have an idea," I say slowly, drawing each word out. "Really, I should charge you for this service, but I'm already here, so . . ."

"Our mom *is* paying you," the one on the left says.

"Not for this, she's not." I wait for their eyes to widen in anticipation, and when they do, I lean close. Their heads duck to mine, and I whisper, "I'm going to give you both . . . MAKEOVERS!!"

I sit back on the couch, bracing for the excited screams I know are coming.

Wait for it. . . .

Um, hello? Screams would be oh-so-appropriate here. Why are there no screams? Instead, both of them have wrinkled foreheads as they look from each other to me.

"Why?" one asks.

"Well, because I'm feeling charitable. Besides, when you have mastered something, as I have, the honorable thing to do is to pay that forward by passing your expertise on to the next generation. I'm pretty sure Martin Luther King said that. Or maybe Lady Gaga. I can't remember, but whatever, because it's solid advice. In fact, consider that life lesson number one."

The girls exchange glances again, and this time the one on the right speaks first. "What do we need a makeover for?"

Duh. "Popularity."

More wrinkled foreheads. What is up with these girls?

"I can show you how to be popular," I say. "I have pre-patented techniques, and before this night is over you could be on your way to owning first grade."

The girl on the left puffs her bangs out of her eyes. "We're in *third* grade. We're not *that* much younger than you."

Well, what a difference a few years make, then, because one of us is going home with cold, hard cash in her pocket, and the other two are obeying the bedtime I enforce. I feel like sticking my tongue out at them, but as the far-more-mature one among us, I resist.

She looks at me. "Most of the kids in our class already like us, because Hope always shares her snacks and I'm awesome at soccer and we're both really nice to our friends."

I narrow my eyes. "Do you want me to play with you or not?"

She glances at her sister, who shrugs.

"I guess," Hope says.

"Perfect. Curling iron. Stat."

"What are stat? I don't think we have those," says the other, who I've figured out is Charity via my superior powers of deduction.

I sigh as if I'm injured. "'Stat' means 'pronto,' 'on the double,' 'quickly.' Do you not watch any medical dramas?" When they look confused again, I wave my hand. "Never mind, just grab the curling iron."

"Um, we don't have that, either."

What is this place? They can afford a forty-seven-thousand-button remote but deprive the women of the household of a curling iron? I shake my head, but I'm not deterred. When it comes to the pursuit of beauty, I never let anything get in my way.

"Okay, grab a whole ton of spoons and some butterfly clamps."

"Some butterfly whatza?"

I throw up my hands. "Just see if your parents have any binder clips, okay?"

Both girls shuffle out of the room, and I pull up the notepad app on my phone. I'm all about making lists, and this project is going to need them. Okay, so now if I start with Hope and give her curly hair and then use a flat iron on Charity's to make it the complete opposite—

Wait, they have to have a flat iron, right? I pause, consider, and then decide that of course they do. Not owning a flat iron would make them literal medieval cavemen.

I get back to my list, and I'm only on item twenty-two when both girls return with the supplies I requested.

I park Hope on a chair in front of me. "Oh, hold on, we need to dampen your hair first. Do you have a spray bottle?"

Hope shakes her head at the same time Charity answers, "Just the stuff under the bathroom sink. But that's for cleaning the toilet."

"Should work fine," I say over my shoulder as I head for the bathroom. I dump the contents into the toilet and flush, then fill the bottle with hot water. Perfect. The first few sprays smell a little chemically, but whatever. I'm sure that'll go away as we work.

I return to the family room and hand Charity my phone. "You sit there and monitor my Instagram. I want real-time updates on any activity. Got it? Take notes for yourself too, because if you want to be popular, you need to master your various app options."

Charity plops down. "Okay, fine, but we can't get cell phones until middle school."

I arch an eyebrow. "You need to start campaigning ASAP. When I was your age, I was sticking Verizon magazine ads to the ceiling above my mom's bed at least four nights a week, tucking brochures comparing cell phone plans under her pillow, taping them to the rearview mirror in her car, rolling some up in her yoga mat . . . you name it. You girls have to start planting the seeds now, because you're already falling behind. That's life lesson number two. You're welcome, and stay tuned; there's more where that came from."

As I talk, I dampen Hope's hair. I'm doing her the biggest favor in the world, and all she can do is complain about her eyes watering from the bathroom cleaner fumes. Fine, so maybe I didn't rinse out the bottle, but stop being such a baby about it—beauty comes at a price! I roll big chunks quickly but carefully around each spoon and secure them with binder clips that mostly do the job. I'm pretty proud of my improvising, I have to say.

When we're done a few nothing-new-on-Instagram minutes later, I use a pillow from the couch to press down on Hope's hair so we can keep all the "rollers" in place as I march us all up to the master bedroom and plug in Mrs. Terzetti's hair dryer. At least she has one of these. Sheesh.

I've barely aimed it at Hope's head when she begins wincing and then screeching, "Ow! Ow! Ow!"

I tap my foot and flip the dryer off. "What now?"

"That's burning my scalp!" Hope yelps.

I turn the dryer over in my hand. "It's only on the medium setting. Don't be such a whiner."

"It's the spoons! They're a thousand degrees."

Ugh. Exaggerate much? Someone needs to tell her that no one appreciates snark. It should be me clueing her in, but I've already given away too many valuable life lessons, and I'm not getting nearly enough idolization in return.

I place a hand on her head and snatch it back just as quickly when it scorches my palm. Huh. "Fine, I'll switch to the low setting, but we have to use a heat source or the curls won't set."

Hope whimpers and Charity opens her mouth to say something, but I cut them both off by holding up my hand. I guess I can offer a few more life lessons, since they so clearly need my help. "Sometimes you have to suffer for beauty. It's a universal truth."

I nod a few times, wisely, but it's wasted on the girls, who seem to be having some weird telepathic conversation with just their eyes. Twins can be so freaky. I should get extra pay for putting up with the creep factor.

Ignoring them, I pick up the hair dryer again and set it to low. At first Hope goes along, but after about thirty seconds she reaches up and begins yanking out the binder clips. Charity abandons her spot on the edge of the tub to help.

I shriek. "What are you doing? The curls haven't set!"

Both girls look at me, and Charity speaks first, "We don't want to suffer for beauty. We're perfectly happy with the way we look."

Hope adds, "And I feel sorry for anyone who has to do all this just to be popular. Ellie always tells us the most important thing is to be kind and smart."

Of course Ellie would say something supercheesy and Hallmark-y like that. I snort. "Ha! Try getting through middle school on those things alone!"

They both look at me with pity, and my jaw drops.

No one EVER looks at me with pity. Is this what it feels

like to be Ellie? Why would they pity me? They should want to *be* me. At the very least they should want to be *around* me.

But then Hope adds, "I really miss Ellie."

And *then* Charity puts her arms around her sister and pats her half-dry, half-curled hair and says, "I know, me too. It'll be next Saturday soon."

WHAT?!? Have I entered an alternate dimension?

At first I'm confused. How is it possible that, even now, they still want Ellie over me? All she ever does is scribble in her journal, which cannot be interesting. I was helping them. I'm the popular, fun one. And Ellie is so . . . bookish. And goody-goody. And helpful. Only parents prefer goody-goody and helpful over fun and popular. Except not all parents. Even though my mom was supernice to Ellie tonight and not so much to me, she could never prefer Ellie over me.

Could she?

I snatch the couch pillow off the floor and flounce out the door (if only they'd shown the least little bit of appreciation, because I have an excellent life lesson on achieving the perfect flounce). I pivot and yell back into the room.

"Why wait for next Saturday? You want Ellie? Let's go get her!"

I head for the steps, not pausing to see if they're following me. But I know they will, and sure enough, by the time I reach the front hall closet they're on my heels. I yank my peacoat off the hanger Mrs. Terzetti put it on and tap my foot as the girls grab their own far-less-stylish jackets (matching, of course) and hideous rain boots, for God knows what reason.

"Where are we going?" Charity asks.

"That's for me to know and you to find out," I snap.

It's only fair that Ellie swap places with me at the dance because she's had her fun by now and she needs to share the wealth. Mom never has to know—we can make the switch back at the end of the night, no problem.

Hmm. I don't have a key to lock up the house (or, more important, unlock it when we get back), but I figure if we go out the garage we can leave the automatic door open just enough to roll underneath. See? I'm thinking of everything here. I should totally take up heist planning as my next hobby.

I lead us wordlessly to the breezeway off the kitchen, where the twins' mom left the house earlier. As we enter the garage, I'm still plotting. As I see it, there's only one possible flaw. The Terzetti house might be only a couple of minutes to the school by car, but that's probably more like an hour on foot.

Unless . . .

I squint at a ride-on lawnmower in the back corner. Hmm. Taking the mower versus walking could earn me tons of bonus hangout time at the dance. This decision is easy-peasy lemon squeezy.

"Hop on, girls," I order, pointing. Immediately, both open their mouths to protest, but after one look at my face, they close them and follow my instruction.

Good. Now, then.

Life lesson number whatever number we're on: Never walk when you can ride. Which is closely related to life lesson number seven: Always make an entrance.

TESS { **7:59 P.M.** }

Tess! Alex singing "Jingle Bells" for an hour. Come save me, pls. BTW, still can't believe M is wearing your dress!!!!

Ugh, Carmen, worse than that. 😠😠😠

What?!? Need detailssssss.

. . . Helloooo?

Tess?

Sry. Had to look for Leif. M thinks he's here with her.

???!!!!

Whatev. Am gonna find him 1st & prove he wants to be here with me.

Of course he does. Just wait till he sees you onstage. 😎

BEST. NIGHT. EVER.

Wish I was there to help. & sing. & not wearing the UGLI-EST dress in the WORLD. 🙁

Wish you were here too.

Enough about my awful night. Need to know. Did you find L yet?

He's hiding behind a fern.

Go get him!

GENEVIEVE { 8:00 P.M. }

THE STAGE LOOKS SO MUCH HIGHER THAN I expected. It's probably not any taller than the one at the mall where we had the Battle of the Bands, but this one looks . . . more dangerous somehow. More exposed. Maybe it's the giant banner hanging across the back, screaming HEART GRENADE in enormous pink letters. Or the guy bustling around the gym floor, tinkering with his super-professional-looking video equipment.

Or maybe it's just that I have to stand in front when we perform this time, right at the edge, without Carmen's flashy outfits and big personality to hide behind. Nothing between me and the crowd but empty air. Nothing to catch me if I fall.

I turn my back on the whole setup, and I have an easier time breathing once I can't see it. I don't have to think about it yet—Heart Grenade doesn't go on for two hours. Until then, maybe I can just hang out with Sydney and pretend this is a regular dance like the ones I've seen in a thousand movies. We'll get some punch, jump around to the music, take tons of selfies, and make fun of the girls who freak out over dancing with boys they see literally every single day.

"Do you want to go to the . . ." I start to say to Syd, but she's not next to me anymore. I spot her a little ways away, huddled in a tight group with Abby, Shanti, and Ilana. I can't hear what they're saying, but the way the four of them keep popping their heads up and ducking them back down reminds me of the prairie dogs I saw at the zoo.

I make my way over just in time to hear Syd say, "Do you think he'll ask me?"

"You could just ask *him*," Abby says. She rolls her eyes like they've had this conversation a million times already.

"Yeah, but I really want him to ask *me*. Like, he might say yes if I ask, but I don't want to make him dance if he doesn't want to, you know? If it's *his* idea, I'll know I'm not forcing him."

"He's totally going to ask you," Shanti says. "Omigod, what if he *kisses* you?"

All four of them squeal, and Syd covers her face. "Do you think he will? I might die if he does."

"In a good way or a bad way?" asks Abby.

"Good. I think. Maybe both? Is that a thing?"

"Who are you talking about?" I ask.

I've been standing right next to her for at least fifteen seconds, but Syd looks at me like she's only just noticing I'm here. "Oh," she says, and her cheeks go pink. "Um. Kevin."

"You like Kevin? Since when?"

All four of them giggle and shush me, even though the music is superloud and there's no possible way anyone could overhear us. "Since, like, *February*," says Shanti. "Where have you been?"

Where *have* I been? Syd never mentioned to me that she liked Kevin. Or . . . what if she did? What if I've been so wrapped up in my band stuff that I don't even remember having this conversation? There's no way I could forget something this important, right? Or am I the worst friend ever?

But then Syd gives me a sheepish smile. "Sorry, Gen. I wasn't trying to hide it from you or anything. It's just . . . you never seem interested in talking about boys and stuff, and I didn't want to make you uncomfortable."

My guilt evaporates instantly, and hurt flows in to fill the empty space. I thought Syd and I told each other everything; we have since second grade, when I confided to her that I'd stolen quarters from my dad's dresser to buy candy. As far as I know, Syd has never liked a *real* boy before, just actors and singers. Maybe I would've felt a tiny bit weird that she was going through stuff I'd never felt myself, but that's no reason to hold back something this big and important. Couldn't she have *tried* to talk to me about it instead of just assuming I wouldn't be able to handle it and finding new friends?

Earlier, when she gave me her necklace, I felt so much better knowing she believed in me. But if she doesn't even think I can handle a conversation about a crush, what else does she secretly believe I can't do?

Ilana gasps before I can say anything. "You guys! He's coming over here!"

Shanti whips around. "Really?"

"OMG, don't look at him!"

Syd's eyes get big and scared, and her hands fly up to smooth her hair. "How do I look? Is my makeup okay?"

"You look great," I say. But I guess it doesn't come out enthusiastically enough, because her gaze skates right past me and lands on Abby, who gushes, "You look so gorgeous! He's gonna freak out."

And then there he is, right next to us, and the other girls part to let him into our circle like it's a choreographed dance. I scoot out of the way at the last minute and almost trip over my own feet, but nobody seems to notice. Syd is staring straight at Kevin, and everyone else is staring at Syd, waiting to see what she'll do.

"Hey," Kevin says.

"Hey," Syd replies, and she sounds so weirdly grown-up, like she suddenly knows how to make "hey" mean forty different things at the same time. When did she learn how to do that, and how did I miss it?

Kevin clears his throat like he's nervous. He's basically the most popular boy in our class, and I've never seen him look hesitant before. "Do you . . . maybe want to dance or something?"

"Sure," Syd says, totally cool. And then she walks off with

him toward the middle of the floor, where a bunch of girls are already jumping around and screaming along to a Katy Perry song. For a minute, Kevin's the only boy dancing, but soon a bunch of the other guys peel away from the sidelines and join in, like he's single-handedly made dancing cool. Syd tosses a bright *omigod, can you even believe this?* smile over her shoulder, and I grin back to show I'm excited for her. But my stomach suddenly starts to hurt, like someone has wrapped their fingers around my organs and twisted hard.

As soon as I let my fake smile falter, a flash goes off right in my face, and I turn to see a boy with an enormous camera. "Photos for yearbook!" he calls, and then he snaps one more for good measure before he turns and speed-walks away.

Not exactly the moment I would've chosen to remember forever.

The song that's playing is fast, and nobody's really touching, even if they're dancing "together." But as I watch, Kevin takes Syd's hand and twirls her around, and then he uses that hand to pull her closer to him. She kind of rests her arms on his shoulders, not exactly hugging him, and moves her hips back and forth. I know I would look incredibly awkward if I tried to do that, but she looks like she's been practicing.

"They are *so* cute together," Abby gushes.

"Seriously," agrees Shanti. Ilana starts snapping photos of Syd and Kevin for Instagram, even though we're too far away to get a good shot.

I force my eyes away from my best friend and pull my own phone out of the pocket of my jacket—maybe Carmen has texted back with some performance advice. But I don't have any new messages, and my background picture—Syd and me eating ice cream at her grandparents' lake house—makes me feel worse. I put the phone away and watch the other people on the dance floor instead, but every single girl is wearing a shiny, satiny dress, and looking at them makes me self-conscious about my outfit again. Although Tess did say she liked my shoes, and she never pretends to like anything she doesn't actually think is cool.

"So, are you supernervous about tonight?" asks Abby, and it takes me a second to realize she's talking to me.

"Oh. Yeah, I guess. Pretty nervous."

"I would be freaking out. I mean, you've never even done this before, right? And you're going to be on TV, where everyone can see!"

The few bites of dinner I'd managed to choke down start

playing musical chairs in my stomach, but I try to look calm. "I rehearsed a lot. It'll probably be fine."

"When my older sister was in the talent show a couple of years ago, she got up onstage and totally forgot all the words to her song," Shanti says. "I'd heard her sing it a million times, and then *bam*, gone! It was like someone erased her brain. She looked like she was going to throw up right there on the stage."

"My little brother did throw up onstage during his school play," Ilana says. "He didn't even have any lines. I don't think it was because he was nervous, though. I think he had the stomach flu."

Shanti wrinkles her nose. "Eww. Did it get on the audience?"

"No, he was near the back. But it got on the kid in front of him."

"My mom always gets really dizzy when she's nervous," Abby says. "One time she was giving a speech at my great-grandma's funeral, and she had to sit down in the middle of it and put her head between her knees. It was so embarrassing."

"For her or for you?" asks Ilana.

"For me," Abby says. "Well, I guess probably for her, too."

What if *I* throw up onstage tonight? What if I faint and

tumble off the edge and break both my arms, and everyone in town sees it live on TV? There's no way I'd ever be able to sing a choir solo after that. I wouldn't even be able to leave my *house*. Dad and Papa would have to homeschool me.

Ilana's telling another story about fainting now, and I wish I could yell at her to stop talking, that this is the worst possible thing she could be doing. But she and Abby and Shanti barely know me, and I don't want them to think I'm some sort of fragile flower who freaks out over every little thing. So I just stay quiet and try to keep a smile on my face. If Syd were here, I know she would tell them to cut it out. But apparently Kevin is more important to her than I am right now.

Then again, it's not performance time yet. Maybe Syd just has so much faith in me that she assumes I'm fine, that I don't really need her yet. Because there's no way she would abandon her best friend for some boy if she knew how much I was relying on her, right?

I fold my fingers around her music-note necklace and hope against hope that when it's time to get up on that stage, she'll be right there, front and center, cheering me on like she promised.

ELLIE { 8:05 P.M. }

"TICKET, PLEASE." ONE OF THE EIGHTH graders is set up at a table with a roll of tickets and a silver cash box.

"Oh." I look around. "I don't have a ticket."

"You can buy one here," he says. "Five dollars."

"My date has mine," I tell him.

"Where's your date?" He's tapping the cash box with a pencil.

"I . . ." I peer over his shoulder, trying to see inside the gym. "I'm not sure. We had a misunderstanding. He may be inside—"

"Sorry," he says. "No ticket, no entrance."

"Maybe I can peek in there to see if he's already arrived?" I take off my gloves and rub the back of my neck, which is starting to feel a little sweaty.

"Sorry," he says again. "No ticket, no entrance."

I open my purse and rummage around inside. "I don't think I brought any money."

"Well, there's nothing I can—" he says.

"I know," I interrupt. "No ticket, no entrance."

"That's right," he says. "Those are the rules. I didn't make them. I just enforce them."

I sigh and lean against the wall next to the ticket table. Kevin's got to show up sometime. Even if he is inside looking for me, he'll come out when he realizes I'm not there.

I've been waiting for a couple of minutes when Mr. Thomas, my math teacher, spots me.

"Ellie!" He smiles. "Don't you look pretty. But what are you doing out here?"

"Hi, Mr. Thomas. My date is inside with my ticket. I'm just waiting for him to come out."

"No need for that," he says. "Go ahead in."

"But he said . . ." I shift my attention to the boy at the table.

"It's okay, Brad," Mr. Thomas says. "I can vouch for Ellie."

Brad shrugs. "Your rules," he says.

"Thank you, Mr. Thomas," I say, and I head inside.

The first thing I notice are the streamers. They're a glorious mix of swirling colors, and I'm sure someone put quite a bit of thought into arranging them just so. They're perfect. Just like this night will be.

The next thing I notice is the noise.

The commotion is even louder than it sounded from the hallway. The music is blaring, and I'm certain that all the kids in this gym (all 152 seventh graders) are talking at once.

I push my glasses up and scan the room. Finding Kevin is going to be like finding a needle in a haystack, but hopefully he's looking for me too. I take a deep breath in and smile. Tonight will be everything I dreamed it would be.

Most of the kids are crammed in the front of the gym, toward the stage, so I figure I'll start in the back, where it's a little less crowded. I weave my way in and out of the sea of familiar faces, but not one of them is Kevin's.

I pass a group of girls I recognize from gym class. One of the girls, Genevieve, has always been nice to me. Maybe I'll ask her if she's seen Kevin. She gives me a friendly smile as I approach. Just over her shoulder, the other girls are staring at a couple on the dance floor. They're pointing and giggling and taking tons of pictures of the couple, who are the only ones slow-dancing to a fast song.

"Hi," Genevieve says.

"Hi," I answer. "I love your hair."

"Oh, thanks." Genevieve touches her braid.

There's an awkward few seconds where neither of us speaks. I don't know Genevieve very well, and it's not like we've ever had an actual conversation, other than to say hi to each other during gym class.

"Ummm," I say, mostly to break the silence. "I was wondering if you've seen Kevin?"

"I'm sorry?" Genevieve cups her hand around her ear and moves closer to me.

"Have you seen Kevin?" I say it a little louder.

At the sound of Kevin's name, the circle of girls that were staring at the dancing couple moves closer to us.

"You're looking for Kevin?" a tall girl, Abby, asks.

"Yes." I nod.

Abby crosses her arms and gives me a smirk. "Why?"

Genevieve opens her mouth to say something, but instead looks down at her shoes, which are green high-tops.

I'm not sure how to answer that question, but I decide it's okay to tell them the truth. They're going to find out soon enough anyway.

"Kevin is my date."

"Kevin is your date?" Abby raises an eyebrow.

"Yes." I smile.

"Did you all hear that?" Abby turns to the kids bunched up behind her. "Kevin is Ellie's date tonight."

All the girls laugh, except for Genevieve. She's still looking at her shoes.

A few of Kevin's friends, including the ones who were at the library with him when he asked me to the dance, walk over.

"What's so funny?" Charlie, one of Kevin's best friends, asks.

"Ellie here was just telling us that Kevin is her date tonight."

Charlie's eyes get huge, and then he doubles over laughing. I'm still not sure what's so funny.

"Oh yeah, he's looking all over for you." Charlie grins.

"I thought he might be." My whole body relaxes. "Do you know where he is?"

Charlie looks over his shoulder at the dancing couple, and I follow his gaze.

And there he is.

Dancing. With Sydney.

And he's not just dancing. He's practically hugging her to the beat of the music. Her arms are on his shoulders, and they're swaying back and forth, smiling at each other.

I squeeze my eyes shut for about thirty seconds in an effort to stop the tears from falling. Just as I open them, Kevin is standing right in front of me.

"Oh, hey, Ellie." A chuckle escapes his lips, like he's trying to stifle a laugh. "Were you looking for me?"

My breathing starts to even out. Maybe this was all a mis-understanding after all. Maybe he was just dancing with some-one else while he was waiting for me.

"Yes," I say, barely croaking the word out.

"I didn't think you'd really come."

"Why wouldn't I?"

Now everyone is laughing.

"You didn't think I was serious, did you?"

"Serious?" I'm not sure what he means by that.

"Yeah," Kevin says. "Serious about asking you to the dance."

My vision starts to dim as my brain finally catches up to the conversation. He wasn't serious about asking me to the dance? This was some sort of joke?

The circle of kids surrounding us is growing, and whispers and giggles are spreading like wildfire. My mind is screaming at me to run, but my feet are glued to the floor. The whole room gets cloudy, and the people around me morph into one big blur.

Genevieve reaches out and touches my arm. She's the only one who isn't laughing. "Ellie, are you okay?"

But I can't answer her. If I talk, the sob that's choking my throat will come out of my mouth, and I can't let that happen. Not here.

"Smile for the yearbook!" Suddenly a flash goes off in my face, and the tears that I was holding in pour out as it occurs to me that this moment—and the reminder of what a loser I am—will be memorialized forever.

The laughing gets louder, and even though I still can't feel the floor beneath me, somehow I manage to turn away from Kevin and all the kids surrounding us and stumble toward the locker room.

CARMEN { 8:12 P.M. }

"COCKTAIL HOUR" AT THIS WEDDING IS quickly turning into "cocktail hour plus another forty-five minutes" to make sure everyone is good and hungry. The doors to the main reception area are closed and guarded by a woman holding a clipboard. She keeps talking into a small walkie-talkie, and I wonder if she's conspiring with someone to make sure we starve.

I'm so hungry that at this point I could pretty much eat anything, but there is no way I'm going to hit up the appetizers that are set out. My brothers have found a group of equally obnoxious boys around their age, and they're crowded around the end of the table. A table that is loaded with gelatina, flan, cheese, fruit, and a giant melting ice sculpture that I think was a dolphin but might also be a heart. At the moment, the boys are trying to see how many black olives they can stuff into their mouths, and let's just say that one of them doesn't have very good luck and his olives shoot out and roll all over the table. Lucas is trying to put a shrimp down Alex's shirt, and I have a feeling that if I come too close, I'll be his next target. So yeah, I'm not about to eat anything here, which means I'm getting a serious case of the hangries (hungry + angry, which is not a pretty combination).

I pull my phone out of my purse (black satin with silver studs—at last I have something cool at this wedding) to check if Tess has gotten back to me, but there's only one bar at the top of the screen. Are you kidding me? Haven't I already been through enough hardships today?

Reception here is awful. Now I can't even talk to you. 🙁
I pray I'll hear from Tess soon.

"Ugh!" I say a bit too loud. Two women whispering near me pause for a moment and glance my way before they begin to talk again. I bet they're discussing my dress. Because how can you not? I curse my awful luck. When I envisioned everyone looking at me tonight, it was up onstage while I rocked out, not because of what I'm wearing here.

A series of sharp, shrill noises fills the room. The woman at the door holds a glass and is hitting it with a knife. I cringe until I realize it's a signal that we can go into the reception area. *Food*, my brain says. *Food*, my stomach rumbles back.

It is pretty much a stampede. I walk through the doors and freeze.

Wowsers.

I thought my dress was awful, but it's nothing compared to this room. I stifle a giggle because the decorations are so not my style. Not that I'm surprised. My cousin Marlena's quinceañera theme was "Under the Sea," and I'm pretty sure she used every seashell in the world to decorate.

But tonight, everything is pink.

And glittery.

And shiny.

And full of balloons.

Hundreds of balloons in all shades of pink. I can't imagine what my cousin's new husband thinks of this. I mean, people say real men wear pink, but do they also smother their weddings in it?

I walk under a giant balloon arch and find myself at a table with place cards. And surprise, surprise, each card is tied to a helium balloon, which hovers above the table.

"Table number twenty-two," I say as I find my card. Maybe this is a sign that the night will get better. Twenty-two has always been my number. After all, I was born on February 22, which is a whole lot of twos.

I head over to the table and instantly want to turn around and walk right out of this place. Because there is nothing lucky right now about twenty-two. Seated at the table are my brothers and their olive-stuffing friends. It appears that my cousin decided it was a good idea to put me at the kiddie table.

The kiddie table!

Hello, even though I'm only twelve, people tell me that I'm very mature for my age. Once when my parents and Alex went to Lucas's hockey game, I stayed home alone and made myself dinner. I also babysit my neighbor's kids at least twice a month and took a CPR class at our rec center.

In other words, I don't belong at the kiddie table.

This is the worst ever.

"No way, no how." I stomp my way over to where my parents sit.

"There's a problem," I tell Mom when I reach her. "A very big problem."

"What's that, *mi pajarita*? What's wrong?"

I shove the card with my table number at her. The balloon bobs violently in the air.

"This! There's been a mistake with the seating chart. I'm sitting at the wrong table. I'm way too old to be with a bunch of little obnoxious kids who think it's fun to have burping contests and food fights. This is horrible!"

"*Relajate*. You're with your brothers; it'll be fine," Mom says as if that's supposed to be a *good* thing.

"Everyone is a million years younger than me," I tell her and stomp my foot. I admit it's a little dramatic, but I'm trying to make a point here.

"Really, Carmen? By the childish way you're acting, it seems as if your cousin put you at exactly the right table."

"Fine. Whatever. You obviously don't care about your daughter's well-being, because I'm pretty sure I'm going to go nuts sitting with all of those kids."

"We'll still love you even if you're a bit nutty," Mom says.

I throw my hands up in the air in frustration. I storm away from her without saying anything else, and I don't even care if it looks childish.

There are three seats left at the table, so I throw myself into the middle one and hope the other two will remain empty so I can be left alone.

"Once I ate a whole stick of butter," says the boy who spat out all his olives on the appetizer table.

The other boys lean in toward him as if it's the most fascinating thing in the world. I, on the other hand, am totally grossed out.

"You did not," Alex says.

"I sure did. Want me to show you? I'll do it again." He picks up the bowl full of tiny pats of butter and begins to unwrap them. When he's got a good-sized pile in front of him, he begins to pop one in after another.

"Anyone can do that," Lucas says. He grabs a bunch of butter pats for himself. He shoves three into his mouth, and the rest of the boys settle in for what promises to be the grossest showdown in the world.

"That's disgusting," I say, because yuck.

"That's disgusting," Alex repeats, making fun of me.

"Stop it!" I snap at my brothers.

"Stop it!" all of the boys repeat back, and I swear, I'm about to get up and walk home even if it takes me a week.

But before I can do anything rash, a hand taps me on the shoulder.

"Oh my gosh! You were in the wedding!" says a girl who looks even younger than my brothers. She sits down in one of the empty seats and stares at me as if I'm some kind of celebrity.

I nod and her smile grows even bigger.

"This is amazing! I can't believe I get to sit next to one of the bridesmaids! My friend Addison is going to flip when I tell her!"

So maybe this isn't Heart Grenade's big concert, but I have to admit, it is kind of nice to be looked at as a big deal, so I smile back.

"I'm Victoria," she says and reaches out and touches the skirt of my dress. "This is so pretty. You're so lucky."

I study her to see if she's joking, but she only smiles at me.

"Thanks," I say, not that it makes me feel much better. She is wearing a poufy dress with tiny hearts all over it, white socks with ruffles, and a purse that is a stuffed animal dog. It has a strap and a zipper across the back to put things into it.

She unzips it and takes out some lip gloss. She holds it out to me. "Want some? It has glitter in it."

"Um, no, I'm okay."

She shrugs and starts to put it all over her lips. I pull out my phone and pretend to be busy.

I have a text, but it's not from Tess. It's from Genevieve. Figures. When I finally get reception, I hear from the one person I don't want to hear from.

You start "Hear Us Roar" really quietly, right? And then you get louder toward the end? Just making sure.

Uh, yeah, that's how *I* sing it. That's why people love the song so much, because my singing gets more and more powerful until I get to the refrain. As if I'm really starting to roar. It's kind of my thing.

Not Genevieve's thing.

I delete her text and type out a bunch to Tess, one right after the other, and cross my fingers that they send.

You haven't forgotten about me, right? ☹

Tess?????? Miss you so much.

You = Best Night Ever 👍

Me = Worst Night Ever ☹

"Is this seat empty?" a voice asks.

Great. The last of the little kids has arrived.

"Nope," I answer, and keep my eyes on my phone.

"Hi, Jackson!" the girl next to me says, and he mumbles

something back to her. It doesn't seem to bother her, because she keeps on talking.

"I know Mom said I have to sit next to you, but is it okay if I sit here instead? Because guess what?" She pauses for what I can only imagine is dramatic effect and then points to me. "She's part of the wedding! How cool is that?"

But if she is looking for someone to share in her excitement, the person next to me is not the one to do it. Instead, he lets out something between a snort and a laugh.

"Wow, real cool. Maybe the coolest thing I've ever heard," he says in that way that lets you know he thinks it's anything but cool.

"Mom said you needed to get rid of your bad mood or you'll be grounded," Victoria shoots back.

Okay, this is getting juicy.

I sneak a peek at this Jackson person, who I discover is not only one of the cutest boys I've ever seen but is also my own age! His brown hair curls slightly around his head and gives him that awesome bedhead look that no boy at Lynnfield Middle could ever dream of pulling off. And I bet if he weren't scowling, he'd have an amazing smile.

"Mom said—" Victoria starts again, but Jackson cuts her off.

"I don't care what she says. She can ground me until eternity. It doesn't matter, since I'm missing the most important moment of my life for this stupid wedding."

Did he say he was missing *his* most important moment?

The kiddie table just got a lot more interesting.

I put my phone down and stick out my hand to introduce myself. "Hi, I'm Carmen Bernal, and this is the worst night of my life too. Maybe we can drown in our misery together?"

When he doesn't react at first, I pretty much want to die of embarrassment. But then his scowl slowly begins to soften as he shakes my hand, and yep, I'm right—he does have a great smile!

I pick up my phone again and send Tess one more quick text.

Me = Maybe Not the Worst Night Ever!!!!

JADE { 8:27 P.M. }

EVERYTHING IS ALL SET FOR THE LIVE feed, so Uncle Garrett is off taking a break and searching for his much-needed coffee. Although where he's going to find that at a middle school dance, I'm not quite sure. I sneak away from the camera equipment to send a very important text.

The eagles have landed.

Within a minute, I get one back from my accomplice.

Isn't that a '70s rock band?

All I can do is shake my head as I answer, **What? It's code, genius.**

Oh, right. Um, little problem.

What kind of problem? 😠

Couldn't hide items as planned.

Why not?! I write, but I don't bother waiting for an answer. Forget it, meet me in the locker room at 9:00 and bring the supplies.

I'm pretty sure this kid needs constant reminders, so I add, And get ready for phase 2.

What's phase 2 again?

I text back one word.

SABOTAGE.

ASHLYN { 8:28 P.M. }

IT'S OFFICIAL: I ABSOLUTELY REFUSE TO be a farmer or a landscaper when I grow up. Or mow my own lawn. Not that any of those things were up for serious consideration before this, but still.

I *thought* it would be totally fun to drive this ride-on mower since it's practically the next-closest thing to a car and I have a countdown clock on my phone tracking the number of days until I can get my driver's license. (For the record, it's 1,245.)

But, yeah, no. Lawn mower does not equal convertible. At all.

We've been motoring for*ever*—okay, so more like twenty-five minutes—and we're still not at my school. Partly because we got off to literally the bumpiest start when I couldn't figure out how to make the grass-cutty blade thingies lift up. When we rolled down the driveway they were trying to slice the top inch off the pavement, and it sounded worse than that screechy cat video on YouTube. And the Brats were no help at all because they just covered their ears and yelled at me to make the noise stop. I'm not being paid enough to get yelled at. Seriously.

It was better on the grass, even though that's still all brown and short since winter is barely over. So we pretty much left a path of dirt behind us on all the lawns we drove through, but whatever. Eventually I worked out how to get the blades up, and now we're riding down the sidewalks all regular, except not nearly fast enough by my standards. Even with the pedal pushed all the way to the floor. Ugh.

Plus, every time a car drives by, I'm convinced it's going to be someone I know. Even though it's dark out now, the streetlights are megabright. And with the way no one goes anywhere these days without their phones, every minivan that passes represents a potential video of Yee Haw Ashlyn poised to go viral. Not. Gonna. Happen.

A few blocks back I took the silk scarf from my neck and

tied it '50s-movie-star-style around my head, but what if that's not enough of a disguise?

Time to ditch Yee Haw Ashlyn for Master Schemer Ashlyn.

"Is that the same golf course that backs up to the middle school?" I call over my shoulder to the Brats, pointing at the rolling hills behind the houses on our left. Shortcut + privacy = genius plan.

"I dunno," one of them answers. "But my butt hurts. Are we almost there?"

Complain, complain, complain. *Obviously* the lawn mower seat isn't designed for three of us crammed one behind the other like this, but honestly, isn't an adventure better than the snoozefest of a Monopoly game they suggested? And I'm pretty sure adventures aren't meant to be cozy and comfortable.

I make up my mind and take a hard left when we reach a strip of grass between two driveways. Both girls yelp as they slide to the right, and Hope, who's just behind me, digs her claws—er, fingers—into my side. I huff out a breath and charge on, heading for the fairways beyond the backyards. Luckily the tree line is the only fence between us and all that green open space. Bring it!

"Just hang on," I order. "We have a couple of hills to get

over on the course and then we'll be rolling up behind the school, I'm mostly positive."

Neither girl says anything, so I assume this is cool with them. We bump through the row of pine trees and then we're on the edge of the golf course. Away from the street it's way darker, but I can see well enough to aim us up the center of the grass toward the tee box at the top of the first tall hill. For a sec I wonder if it's gonna be too steep for the mower, but even though we're not exactly cruising, we eventually putt, putt, putt our way up it.

It's the going-down part that's actually the problem.

From this perspective, I definitely know now that this is the same course that backs up to our school, and when I was a little kid I used to come here for sledding every time it snowed. That means I'm pretty used to zooming down this hill at top speed. I've just never done it riding a giant lawn mower or with two terrified girls shrieking loud enough to summon zombies.

"We're gonna die!" Hope screams right into my ear.

Dramatic much? I mean, we're obviously not gonna *die*. Luckily, being annoyed with them keeps me from getting too scared myself.

But then I see the clubhouse at the bottom, outdoor lights

twinkling and directly in our path, and realize Hope . . . might be right.

Help!!

I slam down the cutting-blade thingies to try to slow us, but I guess those don't work when you're going, like, a bazillion miles an hour. I can't believe I was complaining about this mower moving at the speed of grandma before. I am soooo done with this whole being-responsible thing. Just as we're about to slam into a row of parked golf carts lined up in front of the clubhouse, I pry Hope's fingers from my waist and bail out of my seat, dive-rolling onto the hard ground.

Oooooouch!!!

You know what's extra fun? Lying face-planted in dirt.

I lift my head and peek from side to side. "Brats?" I whisper, straining my ears to hear any response over the weird noise the crashed lawn mower is making. It sounds like a chainsaw and an alien spacecraft mating . . . and then everything goes silent as it completely dies. Great. How much allowance would it take to replace a lawn mower? Although I'm sure the Terzettis have lawn mower insurance, so it's probably not *that* big of a deal.

Um, or maybe they'll be too busy suing me for killing their

kids to even care about a dumb mower. Why can't I hear the twins? Who's panicking? *I'm* not panicking.

"Brats?" I whisper again, a little louder this time.

Off to my left comes a giggle, then two. GIGGLES!! Oh, thank God! I should be annoyed that they're finding all this funny, but even though I didn't sign on for this babysitting gig, I'm not *totally* heartless. I would have felt superbad if anything serious had happened to them.

I sit up slooooowly and shake out all my limbs. I am so getting a bruise or twenty out of this. At least all my body parts seem to work okay, though. I follow the laughter to a golf cart along the row. It has a lawn mower stuck into its front and two laughing girls sprawled across its backseat.

"Are you okay?" I ask. "Did you go flying into here?

Matching smiles and nods.

"Are you okay?" I repeat.

"That. Was. *Awesome!*" Charity says.

I sigh and roll my eyes. Now that we've had our lives flash in front of our eyes they're suddenly on board with adventure?

Whatever. I'm fine. They're fine. The mower is definitely NOT fine, but at least we're close enough to walk to school from here, and I can worry about that death trap more after I've gotten my dance on. Judging by the cracking noises my neck makes when I tilt it from side to side, I should probably stick with the slow songs, even if it means finding a girl to dance with on account of the solemn oath I've taken to never look twice at any boy my age. Too immature. I mean, if you could only hear Kevin try to string together a sentence. Ugh. Or that Leif kid. Even worse.

I reach my arms out to pull the twins from the cart.

"Stay low," I whisper. "There are probably security cameras. We don't want them to get us on tape."

I honestly don't know which would be worse: getting arrested because the cameras busted us or having someone post the video of this night online for my entire grade to see. Guarantee it would get quadruple the views Heart Grenade's TV concert will, and that's not me busting on them at all.

"We have to get where we can press right up against the building so we can't be seen," I state. There are also floodlights mounted in the corners of the building, by the roofline, but they point out at the grounds. If we're directly underneath them, we'll be in the shadows.

So smart of me. See, I *should* totally be a heist planner.

I motion for the girls to crouch alongside me, and we

duck-waddle our way along the row of carts to the end. From there the clubhouse is only about half a swimming pool's distance away.

I peek around the corner, take a deep breath, stand, and sprint across the driveway, tucking myself as flat as I can against the brick wall as soon as I reach it.

After I catch my breath I wave on the Brats.

"But what about the Munchinator?" Hope whines, once she's pressed into place next to me.

"The *what*?"

"That's what Daddy named the lawn mower," Charity says, joining us.

I shrug. No time for that. I'm on a mission now. On the other side of this clubhouse is the course's back nine. Last summer Mom decided I should try to be sporty and learn golf from her, so I happen to know at least two of those holes line up with our soccer fields . . . and I'm gonna find them.

We just have to get around this building without making it onto any security videos. I crane my neck to peer up at the roofline of the clubhouse, searching out any blinking red lights that might signal a camera. I'm guessing they'll be right next to the floodlights, and I edge farther along the wall, keeping my eyes trained on the overhang. I'm seriously so supergood at this spy stuff.

"WOOF! WOOF, WOOF, WOOF, ARF!"

I jump twenty-seven feet into the air.

"Oh my God, oh my God, oh my God—a guard dog!" I yell, turning so fast I crash into both girls and send us all toppling into a pile on the ground.

I detach my limbs from the tangle and scramble to my feet. When I immediately trip on a tree root and fall again, I start speed-crawling on my knees, trying to get as far as I can from the clubhouse as fast as possible. Who cares about getting captured by security cameras when getting captured by a ginormous dog with matted fur and a spiked collar and saliva dripping from his pointy teeth would be a thousand times worse? I hate to admit it, but I would pay about a zillion dollars right now to be on the Terzettis' couch, landing my tiny metal wheelbarrow piece on Boardwalk.

After about ten seconds I steal a glance over my shoulder, because those girls had *better* be on my heels. No way, no how am I going back to rescue them from Killer or Brutus or Fang or whatever that mess of madness is named.

Ummm. They're *not* behind me.

They're still at the corner of the clubhouse, bent over something. What the . . .

I get up slowly and tiptoe back to them, totally prepared to run in the opposite direction at the least little movement by whatever horrid monster their huddled bodies are hiding from sight. I do *not* deserve this night!

"Aren't you just the sweetest, cutest, most precious little thing? Yes, you are," Charity is saying in an icky baby voice.

"Girls! Step away from that . . . that *thing*! He's not a pet; he's a menace. I bet he's been trained to snap your necks in half!" Are they really this clueless?

Hope smirks at me, which makes my blood boil. "Pretty sure that couldn't happen," she says.

She moves to the side so I have a clear view of the beast.

My shoulders slump. The "beast" at the end of a long rope that must be tied somewhere around the corner of the building is a fluffball of fur small enough to fit inside my favorite boho slouch bag. Some guard dog. He's wearing a knit sweater with a snowflake on it, and attached to the fur next to his ear is a tiny blue bow barrette. I'm positive I own the exact same one.

I'm also positive the Brats are never, ever going to let me live down the time I ran in terror from the world's cutest

Pomeranian. Sure enough, they're bent over again, but this time it's not to admire the puppy; it's because they're laughing too hard to stand up straight.

Unacceptable.

So unacceptable.

I cross my arms and tap my foot as I wait for them to wind down. But instead we're all shocked silent when a man's voice calls out in the darkness, one thousand percent too close for comfort.

"Snuffles? Are you barking at squirrels again, my yittle wittle princess? Didn't Daddy tell you to stay nice and quiet out here while I finish locking up the clubhouse for the night? Now where are you, my mini-puffykins?"

"Run!" I screech, turning and bolting for the tree line.

They had just *better* be following this time.

RYAN { **8:48 P.M.** }

I DON'T KNOW HOW LONG I WAS HANGING
out in the hallways avoiding Mariah but it's obviously been
long enough for things to get seriously weird in the gym.
"Weird" as in my math teacher, Ms. Huff, Hula-Hooping in
the middle of the dance floor. "Weird" as in my mom bouncing to the music with a big smile on her face. "Weird" as in
Mariah and Tess locked in a full-on stare-down while wearing
identical dresses.

Even though he didn't seem to want to before, I figured
Leif would have handled all of this by now. Apparently not. I
head back out to the front hallway and track him down. He's

standing next to the entrance to the school like he's planning to run for it.

"Dude!" he calls out when he sees me approaching. "It was getting way intense in there. I had to step out."

"What's the deal?" I ask.

"They found out," Leif says. "All of it. That I said yes to both of them. That I have two dates for the dance. Mariah's been glaring at Tess for the last half hour, but now it's getting real. Tess just walked over there, so I'm going to hide until it blows over."

"So they told you off," I say. Because of course that's what *would* happen if two girls found out one guy double-booked them.

"No, man," Leif says, making a face like that's the dumbest suggestion he's ever heard. "There were glares and sighs, and I swear, I thought they were going to have a dance-off at some point!"

Weird. Just last week, two guys in homeroom liked the same girl, and it was no big deal. They yelled for a second, then got over it. But Mariah and Tess decide to have a stare-off over it?

"I should just go wait it out somewhere," Leif says. "Can

you deal with this? You're Mariah's best friend; she'll listen to you. Honestly, dude, I didn't want to go to the dance with either of them. See what being nice gets me?"

"So you're just going to bail?" I ask, dumbfounded. "Why now?"

"I stuck it out as long as I could," he said with a shrug.

If I keep him here, maybe he'll start to like Tess. Mariah will see it and decide to hang out with me. Maybe she'll even realize she likes me after all.

Not the best plan in the world, but the best I can come up with on short notice.

"I have an idea." I lean over to say it in a superlow voice, as if people will actually overhear or something. "You ask Tess to dance. I'll go talk to Mariah and see if I can calm her down."

Instead of answering, he walks over to the gym door and peeks inside. After a quick glance to confirm that, yes, drama is still happening in there, he shakes his head. His eyes are all huge, like he's terrified Mariah and Tess are going to come after him at any second. How this guy is an honors student when he can't even keep his dates straight is beyond me.

"Come on," I urge him. "We'll go in there together."

After a brief hesitation, Leif follows me toward Mariah and Tess. I can't believe I'm actually nervous about getting in the middle of this. *It's no big deal*, I tell myself. *Just two girls fighting over a guy.* This isn't like me at all. Normally I avoid drama at all costs. I'd rather just hang out or play basketball or something. But I don't want to see Mariah get hurt.

By the time we get to the dance floor, Mariah and Tess are staring in opposite directions. They both look at Leif at the same time.

"Hey, Mariah," I say.

I walk around Tess just as Leif is asking her to dance. She gives him a big smile, and the two of them take off. Before walking away, Tess flashes a look of victory at Mariah.

"Where are they going?" Mariah asks.

Her attention is totally focused on the area just behind me. I might as well not even be standing here. I turn around and watch as Leif and Tess move to the opposite side of the gym and begin slow-dancing.

"I. Can't. Believe. This," Mariah says. She looks hurt. Superhurt. More hurt than I've ever seen her look. I want to give her a big hug, but would she even hug me back?

Okay, this is my big chance. I have her to myself. There

has to be something I can do that will make her see that I'm better than Leif.

"I can't believe he said yes to both of you!" I say. "Who *does* that?"

"I know, right?" Mariah says. "It's the worst thing ever."

Okay, so there are probably worse things, but who am I to argue?

"I'm surprised you let him get away with it," I say, shrugging. I'm trying to sound as innocent as possible. Directly in our line of sight, Tess and Leif are still slow-dancing.

"Get away with what?" Mariah says, turning toward me. Not good. I want her to focus on me, but I also want her to see Tess and Leif getting cozy on the dance floor.

"You know, the whole two-date thing," I say. "He totally played you guys."

I feel a little guilty about saying that. Even though Leif did the wrong thing, he's more of a wimp than a bad guy.

"I mean, hasn't he heard about you and Tess—you know, your *history*?" I continue. "He should've known she was the worst possible person he could have gone with."

That part is true. I mean, if Leif actually paid attention, like I do, he would see that Mariah and Tess have some competition going. If he didn't know it before tonight, it should be obvious now. Yet there he is, dancing with Tess like I suggested. Not just dancing; *slow*-dancing . . . and smiling and talking and laughing like he actually *likes* her. I have to hold in a smile. I feel bad that this makes me so happy.

"Well, he knows now," Mariah says, echoing what I'd just been thinking. "So I guess he realizes he has to pick."

But maybe he already has. . . .

The words stick in my brain. I would never say them out loud. That would hurt her, and I can't do that, even if it might give me a better shot at winning her over. So I decide to take a different approach.

"You should stand up to him," I say. Suddenly, I feel this weird surge of adrenaline, like I'm about to run a mile or something. I realize that I'm hoping she'll go tell Leif off. It's probably wrong, but I can't help myself. "Don't let him get away with it. It will make you seem weak."

I wait a second. It's a long second, and I'm sure I've gone too far. Next to me, Mariah is once again staring at Tess and Leif, who are probably still dancing and smiling or whatever they were doing last time I glanced at them. I can't seem to make myself look away from Mariah to see for myself, though.

"Maybe he just said yes to her because he didn't know *I* was going to ask," she says, her face all scrunched like she's lost in thought. "He didn't want to hurt her feelings by telling her someone better had come along."

It's hard to argue with that, mostly because I agree. Someone better *had* come along. Tess is awesome, but I can't see why Leif would like her more than Mariah. There's no girl in the world as great as Mariah.

While I'm thinking about the next thing I should say, Mariah's face goes from angry to thoughtful. Her eyes are wide and full of life. She's softening. That means she isn't angry anymore, which isn't great for me.

"You aren't going to let him get away with this, are you?" I repeat.

"You're right," she says finally, biting her lip nervously like she always does when she's in the middle of thinking something through. "Maybe I *should* do something."

The way she's looking at me now makes my heart all melty. She needs help in the way only a real friend can give it. I've already shared advice; I have to say something else. Something only a true best friend could.

So say something!

But before I can, she turns back to watch Tess and Leif.

"I'm going to dance with him," she says. "He's *my* date."

"Wait!" I yell as she heads in their direction.

She stops and turns around. "What?" she asks. She's looking at me hopefully, like I may have some brilliant piece of advice that will turn all of this around.

"I'm not sure that's such a good idea," is what I end up saying. "It seems a little . . . desperate."

Yeah, real brilliant there. Way to be a genius and save the day. I watch her closely, hoping I haven't just made her feel bad for what she was about to do.

Now she looks confused. "You said I should go over there and stand up for myself. That's what I'm doing."

"I meant that you should tell him off for saying yes to two dates, not beg him to dance with you," I say.

She laughs. "Beg? Beg? Really?"

"Tell him he messed up," I say. "I mean, who makes two dates to the same dance? That's way wrong!"

She says nothing for a minute, and I worry I've crossed a line.

"Okay, yeah," she says. "He was out of line. But maybe it isn't Leif I need to speak to about this. Maybe there's another way . . ."

For some reason she stops talking. She looks over at the two of them, nods, and walks in their direction.

I don't even try to stop her this time.

"Smile!"

All of a sudden, someone steps in front of me and a bright light goes off. Are you kidding me? This stupid guy with the camera . . . again?

The yearbook photographer grins like he's proud of himself, then runs off. Dude is going to have a wall full of photos of me staring at Mariah with sad looks on my face if he keeps following me around like this.

In addition to annoying me, the flash momentarily blinds me. I can't see what's going on with Mariah and Tess and Leif. It also makes me aware that I'm standing in the middle of the dance floor, alone, staring at the three of them like some weirdo. And my mom is out there somewhere, probably in one of the dark corners of the room. I don't want her to see me alone and decide to come over and talk to me.

The refreshments table! That's a place where people can stand by themselves. Other kids will just think I'm getting a drink for someone. I walk toward the table, still seeing white dots. A cup of punch *does* sound good right about now.

Punch in hand, I spot Leif alone. What's up with that?

"She left with Tess," someone says behind me. The voice makes me close my eyes and say a silent prayer to whoever listens to middle school guys' prayers. *Please don't let this be happening to me.*

I turn around and my fears are confirmed. It's my mom. She's stepped out of her chaperone role to speak to me. I'd thought about asking her not to talk to me during the dance, but it seemed like an insensitive request. So here I am, wishing the dance floor would open up and swallow me whole.

"The girls went that way," Mom says. She points toward the bathroom, then her voice softens. "And, honey, I saw Mariah with Leif. You should probably be nearby when she and that other girl finish their conversation, don't you think? She might need her best friend at a time like this."

As mortifying as it is to have your mom speak to you at a school dance, the woman does have a point. Plus, she was a thirteen-year-old girl once. She understands them. That's something I'll never be able to say about myself. But she doesn't mention my crush directly, so I'm more relieved than annoyed, to be honest.

I head in Mariah's direction and hope for the best.

TESS { 8:55 P.M. }

"MARIAH." THE NAME SLITHERS OUT OF my mouth.

"Tess," she replies.

I cannot believe this. Leif spent forever behind that *Jurassic Park*–looking fern (seriously, it could hide a T. rex), then disappeared completely, and then *finally* made an appearance where he was supposed to—with me.

For a second, I thought he was ready to run off—again—even after he asked me to dance, so I pulled him far away from Mariah so he wouldn't chicken out. He had this look in his eyes when we first started dancing, almost like I was the

Incredible Hulk instead of just Tess. I don't know what happened to the Leif I asked to the dance—the one who talked books and music with me. This guy—the one who said yes to both me and Mariah (which bothers me way more than I'd ever admit to Mariah)—looked scared to death of me, even though he tried to hide it between a tight smile and a fake laugh. I took a selfie of the two of us and couldn't even post it anywhere because of the terrified look on his face. He's . . . not really who I thought I'd be hanging out with tonight. Especially after he agreed to go with Mariah, too. It makes me wonder if I actually like him at all.

But before I can figure that out, I have to deal with Mariah. Who interrupted my time with Leif. She actually had the nerve to show up mid-slow-dance and *insist* that we talk right that very second. She shot Leif her usual *I have to deal with Tess* frowny, pinchy-faced look, then grabbed my arm and hauled me halfway across the gym, toward the doors, until I broke free. And now she's stopped in front of me, hands on her hips. I have no idea why she's standing here, waiting for *me* to say something, when *she's* the one who dragged me away from Leif.

My phone buzzes in my boot. I'm pretty sure it's Carmen,

who I'd much rather talk to than Mariah. I slide it out and check.

It's a picture. Taken really sneakily, if you ask me. There's an adorable guy in the very top corner, and the rest of the picture is of a table.

Jackson!!! ☺

I take my time typing a reply. After all, when your BFF—who is missing the biggest moment of her life—just met a cute guy at the Wedding of Horrors, it's important to be there for her.

When I look up again, Mariah's still staring at me, arms crossed.

"What?" I finally say. She's probably doing this to get Leif to dance with her. And that'll be happening the same day I put on a plain T-shirt and jeans. As in, never.

"I need a minute of your precious time," she says.

"That doesn't mean you can drag me away from *my* date."

"We have to talk."

I narrow my eyes at her. Something's . . . different. Her mouth isn't doing that chewing-on-a-lemon thing it usually does when we're forced to exchange words. She's not looking at Leif, who I've now spotted hiding behind his six-foot-tall friend Chris. What is it with this kid and hiding? His white-blond hair totally gives him away.

To be honest, I'm a little freaked out by this version of Mariah. I don't know what to say to her. Which is probably a first.

She seems to spy Leif with his friends and glares in his direction. I *am* a little curious about why Mariah's looking as if she's ready to rip his hair right out of his head, when only a few minutes earlier she wanted him all to herself. "Can we talk in the bathroom?" she asks.

If I raised my eyebrows any higher, they'd be in my hair. Mariah Wilson wants to chitchat with me in the bathroom. I bet she's actually planning to lock me in a stall and then go running after Leif.

"I'm kind of busy right now. Leif and I are dancing. Or . . . *were* dancing before you interrupted us."

Mariah smirks. "Doesn't look like you're dancing now."

There she is. This is Normal Mariah. This I can handle. "You're just jealous because he chose me over you!"

And just like that, she goes back to this new, nonsmirky, almost *nice* version of Mariah. "Come on." She weaves between some kids who have snagged one of the streamers and are wrapping themselves up in it.

Near the doors, we pass Genevieve, who's tugging on her skirt and looking absolutely miserable. I should really ask her to hang out with the rest of the band someday. Judging from that seriously rocker-cute outfit she put together, she'd probably love going shopping at Second Threads with me and Carmen.

"Tess! Seriously. Are you coming or not?" Mariah's standing right outside the gym doors now, hands on her hips again.

I try to sigh, but it comes out more like a growl. "Wait, locker room bathroom or haunted bathroom?"

"Haunted bathroom. What, are you afraid of ghosts?"

"Whatever." Maybe I just don't like faucets that turn themselves on and off or weird moaning noises that come from somewhere behind—or in?—the cinder-block walls. I don't like to spend too much time trying to figure out exactly what those sounds are or where they come from.

I follow her across the lobby. Mariah pushes open the door, which gives an unnatural creak. The bathroom is stuffed full of girls. Most of them are at the mirrors over the sink, brushing their hair and putting on more lip gloss while the muffled bass from whatever the DJ is playing thumps from outside the door. Mariah grabs my wrist and tugs me to the corner next to the handicapped stall.

"Hey, personal space much?" I yank my arm from her.

She doesn't take the bait. Instead, she gets that softer, *nice* look on her face again. I move a step backward. Something bangs inside the wall by my head. I try to ignore the creepiness and focus on Mariah instead.

"Look," she finally says. "I know we aren't exactly friends—"

I snort.

"But I think we have a common enemy."

Before I can even wonder who she's talking about, laughter shrieks from behind me. I flip around, only to find myself knocked into the pipe-banging wall by my algebra teacher, Ms. Huff. Who is throwing her arms around over her head and doing something with her hips and . . . is that a Hula-Hoop?

Ms. Huff. Is dancing. With a Hula-Hoop. In the bathroom. Badly. Very, very badly.

I glance at Mariah. Her eyes are wide, and then she's cackling. It's contagious, and before I can even piece together what's happening, I'm laughing too.

Ms. Huff winds her way across the tile, that hoop swinging around and around, and just as I think I'm never going to be able to take a breath again, a stall door flies open and a boy—a BOY—jumps right into Ms. Huff's path. He flings a camera up in front of his face and—*snap!*—captures Ms. Huff's sick moves. And those moves? Are definitely sick. Like in a throwing-up kind of way.

"Yearbook!" the boy shouts and dashes from the bathroom. Ms. Huff isn't even fazed. She Hula-Hoops her way out the door—even as half the girls are screaming at the top of their lungs about a boy being in the girls' bathroom—reminding everyone in general to please keep to their own bathrooms.

"I can't . . . ," I barely squeak out. "How did he . . . ?"

Mariah wipes tears from her eyes. "That was . . . not normal."

"I'll never be able to unsee that." I'm laughing again before I realize that I witnessed it with Mariah, my mortal enemy. Not Carmen or my bandmates or anyone I usually laugh with. I push my face back into a scowl, cross my arms, and pretend I didn't just see the weirdest teacher moment of the century or a boy jump out of a girls' bathroom stall. "Why are we here again?"

Mariah straightens up. "Leif."

"Who is here with me," I remind her, even though I'm seriously wishing I'd asked some other guy now. Maybe one who didn't say yes to two girls. Plus, I have to scrunch up my toes when I think about Leif. He stepped on my feet so many times when we were dancing, it was really lucky I was wearing my boots.

She shakes her head. "I figured something out. It doesn't matter which of us asked him first or who he really wanted to go with."

"A-a-and?" The answer to both of those questions is me. Although I'm not entirely sure that I really want it to be now. But I can't say that to Mariah.

Mariah smooshes up her face for a second, like she's about to argue with me. But instead, she says, "You're not getting it, Tess. What matters is that he said yes to you and to me. Doesn't that bother you?"

I blink at her.

Is she reading my mind? Yes, I definitely liked him when I asked him to the dance, but not so much now. As much as I hate to admit it, Mariah's maybe, kind of, a tiny bit . . . right. But the idea of letting Mariah win? *N-O.*

"It might bother me. A tiny bit," I finally say.

Mariah smiles just a little. "It *really* bugs me."

And that's all I need to hear. "Where does he get off saying yes to two girls? What's wrong with him, anyway? Doesn't he have a backbone?" Now that I'm on a roll, it's hard to stop. Except . . .

I tilt my head and study her. "This isn't some messed-up way for you to get me to yell at Leif so he runs to you. Is it?"

Now Mariah blinks at me. And bursts out laughing. Again.

"No! I promise." She gets serious again. "I talked to a good friend earlier. And it took me a little while, but I figured out that I was mad at the wrong person. I shouldn't be angry at you. At least, not for this. *This* is all Leif."

I tap my fingers against the wall (which I swear is making some kind of creaking noise). One, two, three, four. One, two, three, four. It's the drumbeat to the first verse of "Hear Us Roar." Which only reminds me that for a guy who claims to really like Heart Grenade, Leif couldn't have looked more bored when I was telling him about the new songs we've been working on.

I drag up a deep breath, look Mariah right in the eye, and say the two words I never thought I'd say to her: "You're right."

Mariah smiles.

"So what are we going to do about it?"

"I don't know," she says. "But it'll be something he'll never forget."

ELLIE { **9:01 P.M.** }

MY POCKET WATCH SAYS 9:01, WHICH
means I've been sobbing in this locker room stall for far longer
than I'd like to admit. I wish I had my journal with me. I wish
I could unleash all of this hurt onto those tender, understand-
ing pages. I squeeze my eyes shut and, for the millionth time
tonight, relive the most humiliating moment of my life. My
cheeks burn as I remember Kevin's face, his laugh, his words.

You didn't think I was serious, did you?

UGH! Stupid, stupid, stupid me. How could I have been
so naïve?

I thought he was different. I thought he wasn't some dumb middle school boy who only noticed a girl's looks or popularity. I thought someone like Kevin could actually care about someone like me.

I lean against the stall wall and shake my head. Real life is nothing like a Jane Austen novel. Someone with a 4.2 GPA should have known better.

My head is pounding and my heart is broken. I just want to get out of here. I want to go home and crawl into bed. I'll make popcorn and read *Pride and Prejudice* and forget all about Kevin and middle school and horrible dances.

I'll call Dad or Soo-jin to come pick me up. I groan—of course, I'll have to tell them why I'm leaving early. I readjust the beautiful headband Soo-jin let me borrow, and my stomach ties itself in knots. She was so happy for me, and I feel awful that she's going to be disappointed. I grit my teeth as I replay the entire thing over again in my mind. How did I allow myself to fall for this? Oh, Ashlyn will be thrilled to use the most humiliating night of my life against me forever. And I can't even blame her. I deserve it for being so clueless.

I need to find Amanda or Lila. One of them should have

a cell phone I can borrow. The thought of seeing Kevin and company makes me nauseous, but I can't stay here forever. There's another entrance to the locker room from the hallway. Maybe I can find someone there with a phone, and I won't have to go into the gym at all.

I exit the stall and turn the sink to cold and splash water on my face, which is now puffy and red. After I pat it dry with a paper towel, I make my way through the changing area toward the other door.

Whispering comes from behind a wall of lockers. It sounds like a girl *and* a boy! There's a boy in the girls' locker room? What if it's Kevin and Sydney? I duck behind another set of lockers so they can't see me.

"Did you do what I asked for phase two?" the girl asks.

"I keep forgetting what phase two is," the boy says. It doesn't sound like Kevin.

"What is wrong with you?" Her whisper sounds like a hiss. "Phase two is the most important part! Sabotage, remember?"

"Oh yeah," the boy says. "It's all set. I did what you told me to."

"Good. And what's your status on phase three?"

"Phase three, phase three." The boy pauses like he's thinking. "That's the slip-and-slide thing, right?"

"You're finally getting it," says the girl. "Where are the supplies?"

"Oh, right, the supplies," he says. "I forgot those."

"Seriously? I literally just reminded you," says the girl. There's a short pause. "You know what, I'll do it myself. Where are they?"

"They're all in my locker in the gold hall by the gym," he says.

"I have to go check in so no one gets suspicious, but I'll meet you there in ten minutes," she says.

"Got it," the boy says. "Ten minutes."

"Heart Grenade is going down." There's a sharpness to the girl's voice now.

"Oh, they'll go down," the boy says. "It will be epic."

The sound of the locker room door opening and then closing echoes off the walls. I peek my head around the corner to be sure they're gone.

I didn't see who they were, but it sounds like they're planning to do something awful to the band! I look around to be sure I'm the only one who heard the conversation. Sure enough, there's nobody else in here. I bite my lower lip. Should I tell someone?

I sit down on one of the benches and sigh. I just want to go home. I don't need any more drama tonight, unless it's in the form of a book. But if I leave and don't tell someone what I heard, what will happen to the band?

ASHLYN { 9:05 P.M. }

"WELL, THIS IS JUST SEVEN KINDS OF perfect," I state.

There are two possible scenarios going on right now:

A. I was a serial killer in a past life, and now I'm being punished for it;

B. Something horrific is gonna go down at the dance tonight, and I have a guardian angel who is trying to keep me from getting caught up in it.

Because honestly, what other explanation could there be for narrowly escaping a madman who dresses his iddle widdle puppy in snowflake sweaters only to run smack into a creek flowing right between the edge of the golf course and the grounds of my school? A creek that is most likely too wide to jump and filled with rocks just waiting to crack my skull open if I try to leap across and fail.

"Fun!" Charity says and clomps right into the water. It doesn't come up higher than the tops of her rain boots, and she splashes straight across like it's NBD.

Her sister has the same rain boots on (shocker!), so in 2.2 seconds they're both on the other side giving me *Come ON already!* looks.

I . . . am not wearing rain boots. *I* am wearing my brand new Zac Ellingsworth fall collection tall riding boots with a hidden side-zip feature. Their soft-as-that-ridiculous-Pomeranian-guard-dog suede will be *completely* ruined if they get the least little bit wet. I glance up at the school, all lit up and calling to me like I'm Dorothy and it's the Emerald City.

Sigh. Double, triple, quadruple sigh.

The Brats are whispering with their heads tilted right into each other, and I just know they're talking about me. Grr . . . Obviously, I don't care one bit what they think of me, but it's just so *rude*. And insulting. Okay, so I overreacted a teensy tiny bit to that "guard dog"—it doesn't mean they get to make fun of me behind my back.

Well, fine, then. I refuse to give them any more ammunition. I'm doing this!

(But not in my suede boots.)

I balance on one foot at a time to tug them off and tuck my socks deep inside the left one. I *try* to roll up my skinny jeans, but skinny jeans aren't so much made for river-wading scenarios.

Oh well. At least *they're* washable, and I'm way taller than the twins, so it'll probably only be my hems getting wet.

I kiss each boot lightly and wish it safe travels before tossing them as hard as I can at the grassy bank on the other side of the creek. It's too dark to see where they land, but there are no splashes, so . . .

There. One problem solved.

Now to get *me* across. Okay, here goes. I mean, the water can't be *that* cold.

OMIGOD, THE WATER *IS* THAT COLD!!!

I yelp and hop on top of one of the rocks sticking out of the creek, because no freaking way do my toes want an ice bath. Probably there're some skin benefits to one, but—and I never thought I'd say this about any beauty regimen—I'd rather skip it at the moment.

"I'm not sure that's a good—"

I don't hear the rest of Charity's sentence because as I go to put my next foot down it slides along the slippery rock and I flail my arms like an out-of-control windmill and that's not enough to help and I'm losing my balance and I'm falling and I can't stop myself and SPLASH!

I'm on my butt in the creek.

And it's colder than an iceberg mixed with a Popsicle mixed with the look Mom gives me when I threaten to slam my bedroom door in the middle of one of her lectures.

I try to stand up, and fall *again.* The bottom half of me is, like, a thousand percent soaked, and seriously, could this night get any worse?!

The Brats are right at the edge, sticking out their hands to help me up, but no, no, nope, because I can tell—I can just *tell*—that they're trying crazy hard not to laugh at me.

Yeah, thanks. So not helpful.

It's not like I can get any colder or wetter, so I just clomp my way to the other side, gritting my teeth to keep them from chattering and also to keep from screaming, because I am sooo completely done with this mission.

OH. MY. GOD. I have a horrible thought. The worst thought ever.

"My phone!" I yelp, fishing it from my back pocket the second my feet touch dry land.

Sure enough, drops of water slide from the very-black-and-devoid-of-life screen and into my palm.

"Noooooooooooooooooooooooooooooooooooooooooooooo!"

I won't cry. I won't cry. I won't cry.

"Don't worry. Our mom accidentally dropped hers in the toilet and she stuck it in a bowl of rice for two days to dry it out and after that it worked perfectly."

For maybe the first time tonight, I have a warm, tender feeling for Hope. She was very appropriately named, because she's sure dangling it in my face now. Let's just pray she knows what she's talking about.

I say a quick prayer to the phone gods and wrap my phone gently in my scarf, which I cradle in my hands. "Where are my boots?" I ask.

Hope holds one up and points at a clump of tangled sticks that I guess is some kind of bush or something.

"The other one went in there," Charity adds super-helpfully.

I hang my head and take the deepest breath ever before dropping to my knees, placing my scarf-wrapped phone beside me, and crawling into the mess of branches that—oh goody—just happen to be covered in prickers. And burrs! Oww! Oww, oww, oww, OWW! I snatch my boot, back out, and rub my scratched-up neck.

I put on my socks. I'm not sure what to do with the boots. My jeans are so wet they'll soak through the suede from the inside out, but option B is tromping up this ravine and across the soccer fields in just my Snoopy socks. Not only would I ruin my pedicure, but I'd probably get all kinds of cuts and scrapes, and the last four months of sleeping with lotion inside my spa slippers to ensure the softest heels ever would be totally wasted. This is seriously the most impossible decision ever EVER. Feet or boots. Feet or boots.

I take one step in my socks and land on a stick poking up in the dirt, and that decides it. Boots it is. I'll just have to head *straight* for the hand dryer in the girls' locker room!

"Um, you have a little—"

I wave Charity's hand away from my hair and pat my

head in the spot she was reaching for, pulling several burrs and a twig from my perfect blowout.

"There're a few more if you—"

"Let's just go," I reply. What's even the point? I'll fix it all in the locker room, where—I just remembered!—I even have a change of clothes stashed away. (You never know when you might be bored of your current getup by the time afternoon rolls around; I'm all about the post-gym-class outfit change. Really, lots more people should subscribe to this concept.)

I stand and follow the Brats up the bank, but it's slow going because I have to stop every five seconds to try to unstick my sopping jeans from my butt.

"You definitely wouldn't last very long with Bear Grylls," Charity says.

"Who is *Bear Grylls*?"

Hope answers, "He has that reality show where he takes regular people into the wilderness and teaches them how to survive. There was one with this girl and she had to eat ant larvae, and another time they couldn't find water, so Bear drank his own *pee*!"

I hold up my hand as we step onto the soccer field. "You can just stop right there. Yes, being on a reality show is completely on my bucket list, but only one where some superhot bachelor is handing me roses or I get to marry a maybe real/maybe fake prince. That is *it*."

"You're weird," Charity says.

"Seriously," Hope adds.

Seriously?

Seriously?

JADE { **9:11 P.M.** }

IT'S BEEN TEN MINUTES SINCE I SNUCK off to the locker room for the secret meeting. I need to get out of this gym pronto to get the supplies, but I've already used the bathroom excuse.

"Uncle G, I need some water," I say, throwing in a fake cough for good measure.

"Okay, just hurry back," he says. "You wanted to run a camera, and I want to make sure we're ready for the big event."

We've been ready for the last hour, and it doesn't start until around ten, but I leave that part out and instead go with a cheerful, "Of course. I can't wait."

On my way, I text.

The one thing my accomplice has done right is some pre-dance recon work to find everything we need. I hide around the corner from his locker so no one will see me as he collects the bags of liquid soap that are *supposed* to be used as refills for dispensers. They're clear, like those saline bags that hang in emergency rooms on hospital TV shows.

"Almost done," he whispers.

"Hurry up before someone sees you," I say.

"These are slippery," he says as he shoves the refills in a small backpack. "I'm going as fast as I can."

I run over to his locker to help him load up. Once it's full, I grab the bag. "I'll go stash this until it's time. Which one did you say is open?"

"Forty-three," he says, shoving a small tripod out of the way before closing his locker.

I can't be gone much longer or my uncle will wonder where I am. An extended water break could look suspicious.

"Got it," I say. "Watch for my text. It's almost time."

He nods, and I take off down the hall, avoiding all eye contact with the kids coming in and out of the hallway. The girls' locker room door squeaks as I push it open. I poke my head

in to make sure no one is in there. It looks clear, although . . .
is that the sound of footsteps? If someone's in this room right
now, it could ruin my whole plan. Why couldn't my accomplice have remembered the supplies earlier?! My heart beats
faster, the thumping making my ears pound. I quietly tell it to
shush. I don't have time to be nervous.

I head over to the attached bathroom to make sure I'm
alone. I lean down and check for feet under the stalls. All
good.

I find locker number forty-three. It's open and empty like
it's supposed to be. The backpack fits inside without me need-
ing to shove it. Perfect. I'll come and get it right before the big
event so that I don't risk getting caught with the evidence.

I shut the locker door and walk toward the exit, and that's
when there's a *clink-clink* sound like something dropped to the
floor. I do a quick scan around the lockers, but there's nothing. It must be my nerves playing tricks on me. I need to get
back before Uncle Garrett sends a search party out. Or worse
yet, suspects I'm up to no good. I mean, *figures out* I'm up to
no good. Nothing is going to stop me from taking this band
down tonight.

When I get to the gym, there's a whole lot of noise near the punch bowl. As in, much more noise than normal from a room full of kids and loud, blaring music.

"What's going on over there?" asks Uncle Garrett.

"I have no idea," I answer. "Want me to check it out and get some photos for the website?" He nods, and I head over to see what all the commotion is about.

Some kids are freaking out. Some are laughing. More and more are running over as the crowd around the punch table gets bigger and bigger.

"Are you saying my teeth are *green*?" one girl asks.

When she opens her mouth and has her friend inspect them, I manage to snap a picture.

"I'm saying they match your dress," says one of the boys as he and his friends bend forward, laughing hysterically.

A group of girls runs off, quite dramatically I must say, screaming about how their whole night is ruined. *Yeah, your whole night is ruined because of something in the punch.*

I smile. *Just wait, girls. I'll show you how to ruin someone's night.*

TESS { 9:19 P.M. }

SOMEDAY, WHEN HEART GRENADE IS PLAYING
Paris and Beijing, we'll have a real backstage area with dressing
rooms and comfy sofas and bowls of M&M's with all the ugly
brown ones picked out for us. Today? We have the chorus
room. And no M&M's.

But it doesn't really even matter, because the second I walk
in, the excitement and the nerves hit me harder than that ocean
wave did last summer in Florida.

"Whoa," Mariah says. "It's intense in here." We were right
in the middle of discussing our very important plans for Leif
when it was time for me to meet the band. So I told her to

come with me, even though she reminded me—for the hundred thousandth time—that she doesn't even like our music. So I reminded *her* that there's no way we can plot revenge if we don't talk for the rest of the night. And then she heaved this enormous sigh, like I was making her give up the night of her life or something, and followed me here.

"It's always like this before we go onstage," I say, except that it's way more so tonight. "Come on."

Mariah trails behind me as I weave past the piano and the music stands to say hi to Claudia, our guitarist, and Faith, the bassist. Genevieve's off practicing in a corner with her eyes closed, so I don't bother her. Kate, the fill-in backup singer, shouts my name and wiggles her fingers at me. I don't know her very well at all. She's a sixth grader Faith asked to step in just for tonight to take Genevieve's usual spot.

Claudia's eyes flick between me and Mariah. She adjusts the stretchy black-and-silver top she's wearing and raises her eyebrows at me.

I nod at Claudia at the same time as Mariah whispers, "You sure it's okay for me to be here?"

"Yeah. She just wants to make sure it's okay with *me*." The feud between Mariah and me is legendary with the band.

"Legendary" as in: They don't really want to hear about it anymore.

"I'm going to grab a drink," Kate says. "You guys want anything?" Everyone shakes their heads, and Kate flies out the door to the hallway.

I pull the drumsticks from my boot and set them on a chair. Then I fish out the bright lipstick my mom hates (also in my boot—really, who needs a purse?) and make my way to one of the mirrors. There are a lot of mirrors in this room. Apparently, the kids in choir like to look at themselves when they sing.

I trace my lips and wonder what Carmen's doing right now. That's another thing we won't have to deal with when we're big-time famous—parents making us go to silly things like weddings instead of our own concerts. As I cap the lipstick, something starts tapping behind me.

In the mirror, I can see Mariah. She's picked up my drumsticks from the chair and is rapping out something on the piano bench. I whirl around. My first instinct is to snatch them away—because *no one* touches my drumsticks, especially not the girl I've been at war with since second grade—but I pull my hand back. She has no idea I'm even paying attention, and there's something in her face . . . but I can't figure out what it is. She's not very good at drumming, that's for sure. Her rhythm is totally off, and her arms are all stiff as she slams the sticks down over and over again. I don't even recognize what she's trying to play until she starts humming under her breath, so quietly I can barely hear her.

It's "Hear Us Roar."

I just stand there and blink as she bangs away. She's totally oblivious to everyone else. Almost like she's working through something in her head and isn't even aware of what she's doing.

Mariah Wilson. The girl who tried out for my spot in the band and lost. The one who then told everyone who would listen that Heart Grenade was a just a wannabe school band with generic songs and talentless musicians.

Huh.

"Hey," I say, really quietly.

She stops, swallowing the song and thrusting the drumsticks at me. "Um, sorry."

I want to tell her that no one touches my drumsticks. The words are just about to fall out of my mouth, but I clench my jaw shut. For some reason, I don't feel like saying that to Mariah right now.

I drop the drumsticks back into my boot and decide to completely change the subject. "I think we should go with option B," I finally say, as though the drumming thing never happened. "It has a much higher probability of embarrassment." If we really are going through with Operation Make Leif Regret His Life Choices, it needs to be something he'll never forget.

"But option A will be easier to execute." Mariah puts her hands on her hips and gives me that competitive (and annoying) Mariah Look I'm used to. Which is much easier to deal with than drumming Mariah. Or nice Mariah.

"We need to be able to get in and out quickly, and we can't do that with A." I stride past her, back toward the other girls.

"Yes, we can, as long as we stay focused," she says as she runs to catch up with me.

"I don't think we can—"

"Picture time!" Faith shouts from across the room. It drowns out Claudia's guitar and Genevieve's vocal scales.

"Where's Kate?" Claudia asks.

"Here! I'm back. Sorry," Kate says from the door. "I was trying to find that yearbook guy to take a group shot of us. But of course he's nowhere when I actually need him. Can you believe he actually took a picture of me trying out Ms. Huff's Hula-Hoop earlier? Ugh!"

"I'll take the picture," I say.

Mariah stands off to the side as all of the band members crowd in for a giant selfie.

"Are you coming?" I ask Genevieve.

She looks super freaked out standing in front of the vivid red LYNNFIELD SHOW CHOIR NORTHEASTERN OHIO FOURTH RUNNER-UP banner. She finally nods and perches herself on the piano bench next to Faith. I hold out my phone as far as my arm will go. If Carmen can't be here, the least we can do is send her a picture and let her know how much we miss her. But I can't get everyone into the shot.

"Gen, scoot closer to Faith," I order. "Claudia, duck your head."

Genevieve inches toward Faith. "Sorry," she says for no reason at all.

Faith grins and slings an arm around her shoulders. Claudia slouches down. And I still can't fit everyone in. Unless we want to send Carmen a picture that has my head cut off. And that can't happen, because these purple streaks need to be preserved for posterity.

"I'll take it," Mariah pipes up.

"Um . . . okay." Considering how Mariah doesn't exactly love the band—or, at least, how I *thought* she didn't love the band, until I heard her humming one of our songs—I have no idea why she'd volunteer. But then again, I guess anything is possible with her tonight.

I hand her my phone, and she steps back to get everyone in the shot.

"Ready? One, two, oh my God!" Her face contorts into a look of horror.

"What?" Claudia jumps out of the shot. "Is there a spider? Please say there's not a spider." She's pulling her stretchy top away from her stomach, like she's sure she'll find a brown recluse hanging from it.

"No," Mariah says. "It's Kate. Her teeth are green!"

Kate slaps a hand over her face and runs to one of the mirrors. She opens her mouth and shrieks. Sure enough, her teeth are pea green.

"What did you *do*?" I ask.

Kate scrubs at her teeth with her hand, but that green isn't going anywhere. "I don't know! They looked fine when I fixed my makeup. And all I did after that was get a cup of punch."

"I knew it!" Faith says. "I thought I saw some of the guys acting shady over by the punch bowl. They were totally up to something."

"I can't sing like this!" Kate says. "Everyone will laugh at me. It'll be on TV! They'll put it all over YouTube! I'll be YouTube famous for having *green teeth*!"

My heart practically stops. "You can't drop out *now*."

"Please don't," Genevieve adds. She looks about ready to puke in the trash can.

"Guys, I can't. I am *so* sorry. I have to go home before anyone sees me." And with that, Kate dashes out of the chorus room.

Faith throws up her hands. "What are we going to do now? We're on in an hour, and we don't have a backup singer!"

"I'll go see if I can find Abby," Mariah says. "She was great in *Carousel* last fall."

"But she doesn't know the song," Claudia says.

"We're totally doomed," Faith adds.

Genevieve doesn't say anything. But she's holding a hand over her mouth. This is so not good.

"We need someone who knows the song and who can at least stay on pitch," I say.

Mariah nods. Then her face practically lights up. "I can do it. I can sing."

"You?" I ask. There's no way. I've never heard her sing. I mean, she was humming earlier, but that doesn't really count.

"You don't believe me, do you?" Her mouth curves up into a smile.

"Even if you can sing, you'd have to know all the words to our song," Faith says.

I turn to my bandmates. "We're just going to have to make do without a backup singer. Maybe no one will notice." Which I know is a lie. Everyone's going to notice. They might not be able to figure out what's different, but they'll be able to tell that there's something off about the song.

This is a complete disaster.

"We don't really have—" Claudia's saying when from behind me, someone bursts into the opening lines of "Hear Us Roar."

I spin around. It's Mariah. Her hands are lifted slightly in front of her, almost like she's going to rest her fingers on piano keys, her eyes are closed, and she's singing *our* song for all she's worth.

And, ugh. She's good.

Really good.

It takes almost a full minute before I can stop staring at her long enough to glance at Faith and Claudia. Faith gives me a thumbs-up, while Claudia's mouth just hangs open. Behind Claudia, Genevieve is grinning.

Mariah comes to the end of the song and opens her eyes.

"How? Why? When?" are the only words I can get out of my mouth.

She shrugs and looks down at her feet. "Your songs aren't all that bad."

"Wait, you know more than just 'Hear Us Roar'?" Faith asks.

Mariah nods. "I know them all."

I start tapping out a rhythm on my leg. "But you hate Heart Grenade. You've told me that about nine hundred times."

Mariah shrugs again. "I . . . well, I wasn't really happy that you got in and I didn't. But you know how that is." She looks right at me when she says this last part. I know she's talking about our rivalry, and she's right. I do know.

"You're not exactly an amazing drummer," I say.

That pinchy-faced look comes back right away, and I hold up my hand. "But you've got a great voice." I press my lips together, take a huge breath, and then say, "You want to be our fill-in backup singer tonight?"

The moon has fallen from the sky, and Leif's probably going to apologize for being a complete jerk, because I just did the unthinkable.

I asked my mortal enemy to join my band. Temporarily, but still.

Her puckered mouth drops. "Are you serious?"

"You heard me."

She smiles. A real, happy smile, not a Mariah smirk. "Absolutely. I'm in."

"Okay. Good." I pause for a second as she smiles even wider. "Don't let it go to your head."

I don't have to look at her to know she's rolling her eyes. Mariah's eye roll practically comes with its own sound. A screechy, nagging, eardrum-piercing sound.

"Are you sure about this, Tess?" Claudia asks. "I mean, Mariah's great, but—"

"Sure I'm sure. We need someone to take Kate's place, don't we? And Genevieve can help her." I grab Genevieve by the elbow and pull her over to Mariah. "Right?"

"Um, okay," Genevieve says in a small voice. "I guess I

can tell you what parts you need to come in on."

"Wait," Mariah says. "I'll sing with you guys. But only if Tess agrees to do option C."

"Option C?" Faith asks. "What's that mean? That's not one of our songs."

I don't answer her. Faith is one of my best friends, but right now, Operation Make Leif Regret His Life Choices is classified information.

"What's option C?" I ask her. "I don't remember talking about an option C. And besides, *you're* the one who asked to join us in the first place!"

She gives me an evil grin. "It's good, I promise."

Weirdly, I believe her.

"And I'll tell you in a minute," she says, "after Gen shows me where to come in. And after we get our picture . . . I mean, after you all . . ."

"Don't be ridiculous. Of course you can be in the picture," I say.

"Really?"

I smile back at her. It feels weird, but I can't help it. "But you have to stand in the back, because we're wearing the same dress." At least no one will be able to tell we're wearing the same thing on TV, since you can't see much of me besides my head once I'm behind my drums.

Mariah rolls her eyes, but she stands in the back anyway. As we squish together for the picture (with everyone's heads in the shot this time), I get this humming, excited feeling deep in my stomach. I give the photo the perfect caption before I send it off to Carmen:

To rhythm, rock 'n' roll, and revenge.

CARMEN { 9:19 P.M. }

THE FIRST TIME TESS AND I JAMMED together, we instantly knew it was meant to be. It was one of those moments where everything falls perfectly into place and you're like, *yep, this feels right.*

And tonight, that perfect feeling is happening again. I'm a firm believer in karma, and the fact that Jackson sat down next to me was like the universe saying, *Here you go, Carmen. I know I've sent some doozies your way today, so let me make up for it. I'll place you next to a supercute boy.*

That has to be what happened, because really, what are the odds that the two people who have totally legit and mega-important reasons to not be here would end up sitting by each other?

Yep, that's right. Jackson is miserable too, and his story is as tragic as mine.

"This is the first time in fourteen years my school's basketball team has made it to the state championship, and instead of playing, my parents made me come to this wedding. It's my stepdad's brother's son who's getting married. I've only met him a few times in my life, but my parents insisted we had to come," Jackson told me after I filled him in about my missing out on Heart Grenade's big night.

Mom walks by with a drink and gives me a cheerful wave. I don't know what she is expecting back, but I doubt it's the angry scowl I give her. I turn to Jackson and say, "Parents don't get it."

"Yep, you're right," he agrees. "I begged my mom and dad to let me stay home with one of my friends so I could play in the game, but they wouldn't budge. My mom said family was more important than a basketball game. I told her I know that. That's why I live with them and not at school in the gym."

"Obviously, your mom doesn't know what she's talking about. Take exhibit A." I point to the other end of the table, where Jackson's sister has joined the rest of the kids. Dinner is over, and while the adults may be calmly drinking coffee, I can't say the same for the kids at our table. They all crack up at Lucas as he unties the knot on a balloon and sucks some helium out. He sings "Here Comes the Bride" in a high-pitched voice that sounds like a chipmunk.

Jackson and I let out big, giant sighs, because really, what's there to say when you have to deal with a night like this?

"Are you getting any messages?" I ask when Jackson checks his phone, and he shakes his head. "Me neither. The last message I got was a totally confusing picture from my friend Tess with her and the band and a girl that she absolutely hates. My phone's reception is so bad in here that it takes forever to send a message, and there's no way I'll be able to watch my band's performance on FaceTime like I arranged with one of the girls who is in choir with me. And my mom said there's no way she's paying for me to use the hotel's Wi-Fi since we're here to 'spend time together as a family.' This is truly an American tragedy."

"What if I told you it didn't have to be?" Jackson asks.

"Um, how?"

"I have an idea that I'm pretty sure will work."

"You do?"

"I do." He smiles so big you'd think he discovered how to create world peace. "Didn't you say your band's performance was going to be streamed live on the news station's website?"

I nod, still not quite sure what he's getting at.

"That's the solution!" He looks so excited that I'm sad to crush his bubble of happiness.

I hold up my cell phone. "Didn't you hear me? I have the slowest connection in the universe. The show will be over and my family will be back home before it's even finished buffering."

"We'll find the hotel's business center."

"The what?"

"The business center. Most hotels have one; that's what my dad uses when we travel and he needs to print documents from work. All we have to do is find it, and we're good to go."

"You're a genius!" I say, because he kind of sort of is.

Jackson shrugs like it's no big deal. But it's a *really* big deal. I'm going to get to see Heart Grenade play after all!

The two of us weave through the tables as we dodge floating balloons and try to leave unnoticed. Luckily, La Vibora de la Mar has started, and a ton of guests are holding hands and looping around my cousin and her new husband. It's one of my favorite parts of a Mexican wedding, and even though we need to get out of the room, I have to stop for a second to watch because everyone is having so much fun. There's a part of me that wants to join in, but we don't have much time before the band performs.

We make it out of the ballroom and stop where "cocktail hour and a half" was. Stray olives lie on the ground, and I'm so glad we aren't at the kiddie table anymore.

Jackson stands in the middle of the room and slowly turns in a circle.

"Okay, if I were a computer in a business center at a hotel, where would I be?" he asks.

"Really? You're trying to get into the mind of a computer? You sound like my mom when she loses her keys."

"Obviously, your mom knows how to find missing items. I need to channel the computer and become one with it."

"Right. Sure." I choke down a giggle because I can't really tell if he's joking or not. His face is all serious as if he's deep in thought, with his eyes closed tight and forehead wrinkled.

"While you're doing that, I'm going to try my own method." I walk right up to one of the workers who's picking up empty glasses and tap him on the shoulder.

"Excuse me, sir, I need to send a very important e-mail. Can you direct me to the business center?"

He looks at me like I'm nuts, which I kind of am, but only because time is ticking. "Everyone in the world has smartphones, so they got rid of the business center. Now it's a Starbucks."

I send up a silent curse to coffee drinkers everywhere and stomp back to where Jackson is standing.

"Well, that was a bust. They don't have a business center here."

"No problem," he says with that goofy grin on his face, but he's wrong. It *is* a problem. The worst problem in the world. "I found a hallway labeled STAFF ONLY. There's bound to be a computer there. And the staff will already be connected to the Wi-Fi, so our plan will still work. Trust me, I have this all under control."

Before I can argue with him, he gestures at me to follow him down a hallway that is most certainly not for guests. The doors are labeled with signs that say things like LAUNDRY and LINENS.

Jackson opens a door, peeks his head in, and then closes it.

"Come on," he says. "I'll take this side and you can take the other."

I follow his lead, but not one of the rooms I check has a computer.

We only pause when a woman wearing a hotel uniform walks past us.

"Can I help you?" she asks, and my heart freezes. This is it. We're caught. I'm going to miss my chance to watch the performance.

"Yes, my mom sent me down to get some extra shampoo. She's almost out," Jackson says in a very adult-sounding voice.

"Certainly," the woman says and walks into a room full of toilet paper, towels, sheets, and tiny bottles. She hands him three. "Tell your mom if she needs anything else, all she has to do is call. We'll run it up so you don't need to come down."

"Thank you, ma'am," Jackson says, and the woman nods and heads off down the hall.

I let out a nervous laugh when she's gone. I can't believe she bought that. Jackson is a genius.

"Okay, we need to get moving and check the other side of the reception hall," he says. "Time's running out."

The two of us creep ninja-style through the rest of the

hallway. We open and close doors along the way. We find a room full of helium tanks, one with DJ equipment, and one where the photographer's assistant is taking a break and eating a sandwich. What we don't find is a room with a computer.

"There has to be one somewhere," Jackson says. He opens the door to a big mess of wedding odds and ends.

"Nothing but a bunch of junk." I pick up a bedazzled tablecloth and wrinkle my nose. *What's up with this place? Do they specialize in tacky weddings?*

We step back outside and head to the last door. The only one we haven't opened. It *has* to have a computer. I take a deep breath, say a silent prayer, and put my hand on the knob. Except when I go to turn it, it doesn't move.

"It's locked," I say.

"A locked door is exactly what we're looking for," Jackson says. "That means they have something in there that's valuable, that they need to keep safe."

"A locked door also means we can't get into it."

"You think? I wouldn't be so sure of that. . . ." Jackson pulls something out of his pocket. When he begins to play around with the knob, I fidget as I look around.

"I'm not sure you should . . ."

The door flies open, and my eyes widen.

"You broke into a locked room!"

Jackson gestures inside. "A locked room with a computer!"

"No way!"

I peek around him and, sure enough, he's right. It's a messy office, with papers stacked all over the desk and chairs, but it's an office. And sitting on the desk is a computer. I pretty much want to weep at the beautiful sight. Instead, I run over and shake the mouse, and luck is on our side—the screen lights up!

"This is a miracle," I tell him. "How in the world did you do that?"

"A good magician never reveals his secrets." He walks over so we're standing shoulder to shoulder. I consider throwing my arms around him because he's amazing. But he's also supercute, and I may have enough guts to stand up onstage and sing in front of a room full of people, but I sure as heck don't have the guts to hug a boy I met only an hour ago. So instead, I hold my breath as I search for the news station's website. When it pops up and the screen running community news items appears, I allow myself to completely relax.

We did it!

I'm about to watch Heart Grenade's big concert! With Jackson! Life is finally going my way.

Wait a minute.

I'm about to watch the concert with *Jackson*.

A boy who's not only supercute but is also supernice and wants to hang out with me.

What if he doesn't like Heart Grenade?

What if he thinks we stink?

Or he might even decide that the horrible wedding was more fun than this.

Oh my gosh, what was I thinking? How can I sit next to him during this?

My stomach has that flip-flopping feeling I get before we perform, but this isn't jitters from excitement; these are from fear. I may not be the one singing tonight, but it's still my band's song. If LeBron sat on the bench during a game, he would still want his team to do well, right? And with Jackson next to me, it seems even more important for my band to do well.

"Are you sure you're interested in this?" Because maybe he'll back out. "Heart Grenade is still kind of new. I mean, we're not pros yet or anything."

I click on the mouse to minimize the page, but Jackson places his hand on top of mine to stop me.

"It's pretty cool that you actually wrote a song. My friend's band only plays covers," he says.

My face heats up as I try not to die from excitement, because I'm pretty sure that Jackson is flirting with me. Thankfully, before I can figure it out, he pulls his hand away and jumps up.

"I've gotta get something really fast. Don't move; it'll only take a minute."

I don't even have time to respond. He jumps up and slips out the door before my brain can comprehend what happened.

My eyes go back and forth from the door to the computer screen as I wait. I've almost convinced myself that he's changed his mind and doesn't want to listen to my band when he returns. He holds a plate high in the air like a trophy.

"Look what I scored! I tried to take two pieces, but some lady with a headset was not about to let that happen. We have to share, but it's *tres leches* cake, and it looks incredible. I figured half is better than nothing."

"I don't mind sharing," I say, and I take the fork he holds out to me. I immediately take a bite because living with two brothers has taught me how fast I need to be when boys and food are involved. It's sweet and moist and amazing, and Jackson better hurry up, because I'm not sure I want to share anymore!

"Hey! Wait for me." Jackson pushes my fork away so he can take some for himself.

The two of us settle in behind the desk and pass the cake back and forth as we wait for Heart Grenade's performance to start. We're both eyeing the last bit of the cake when the office door flies open. Before we can do anything, my brothers burst into the room.

"We found you!" Lucas yells while Alex smirks, obviously delighted to stumble upon me doing something that could get me into very deep trouble. If tattling were a competitive sport, Alex would take home the gold.

"Get out!" I yell, not that it makes any difference. Discovering me in here is like winning the lottery. My brothers are going to milk this for all it's worth.

"Mom and Dad are going to kill you when they find out you sneaked into someone's office," Alex says. "With a *boy*."

My face begins to heat up, and I most definitely don't look at Jackson to see what he's thinking about all of this. Leave it to my brothers to embarrass me every chance they get.

Alex is waiting for me to get upset, but I'm not going to give him the satisfaction. Not after everything I've sacrificed to be here and everything I've had to put up with tonight. I'm done with my brothers and their never-ending quest to make my life miserable. Done, done, done.

I step up to the two of them and stand as tall as I can, so I look all big and tough. Well, as big and tough as it's possible to look in this ridiculous dress.

"First," I say, "I'm here to watch Heart Grenade's concert, and Jackson wanted to see it too. Second, if we broke in, then you did too, because you're standing in here with us."

"We were trying to find where you snuck off to. We aren't breaking in," Alex shoots back.

I shrug. "If you say so. Try explaining that to Mom and Dad."

Alex opens his mouth to argue, but before he can, Lucas shouts, "Look! You're on TV, Carmen!"

I turn to the computer screen and he's right. There's a picture of the Battle of the Bands on the site to promote Heart Grenade's upcoming performance. A tiny pang of sadness grips me, because this night is so big for them and I can't believe I'm not there.

"Can we stay? Please?" Lucas begs. "I promise we won't say anything to Mom and Dad."

I let out a sigh of frustration. *Why do my brothers have to ruin everything?* But it probably will be easier to let them stay, because if I kick them out, I'm almost certain they'll run right to Mom and Dad.

"All right," I finally say. "But you have to be quiet."

"We will," Lucas says, and Alex nods in agreement.

I'm not completely sure I can trust them, but something has to go right for me tonight, doesn't it?

I pull out my phone and send a quick text to Tess.

You're going to be AMAZING! You own that stage! Wow them all!

I cross my fingers and hope for good reception so it reaches Tess before showtime.

My brothers bump into me as they try to get closer to the computer screen, but it doesn't matter. In fact, right now nothing else matters, because my girls are about to make history and rock Lynnfield Middle School!

GENEVIEVE { 9:46 P.M. }

I CROUCH ON THE SCUFFED TILE FLOOR of the haunted bathroom, sweaty hands gripping the toilet seat, face hovering above the antiseptic-blue water. My stomach is churning, but I can't tell if I'm actually going to be sick or if I only think I am because Abby and Ilana and Shanti put the idea in my head earlier. It's probably not even possible to throw up when you've only had three bites of food the entire day. I certainly hope it's not, because there are tons of girls in this bathroom, swapping lip gloss and shrieking as the automatic sinks turn on and off at random. Gossip travels at light speed around here, and if someone hears me puking, literally everyone will know about it in five minutes. I want the rest of my class to see a fierce, confident singer when I get up onstage, not a sick girl to be pitied.

I know I need to go back to the chorus room; Mariah's waiting for me to teach her the backup part to "Hear Us Roar." She's way more unprepared for this performance than I am. But I'm not ready to leave this stall yet. Maybe I'd feel a little better if Sydney were here to guard the door and pass me wet paper towels and mints, like she did that time I freaked out before our debate for history class. But she's off doing other stuff, like she has been all night.

One dance with Kevin turned into two and then four and then six. Then there was a fifteen-minute girl huddle, which was mostly Abby, Shanti, and Ilana repeating, "Oh my God, can you *believe* Ellie actually thought Kevin was her *date*?" and cackling hysterically. Syd didn't really seem to think it was funny either, but it's not like she backed me up when I chimed in from just outside the circle and said I thought it was mean. And when Kevin came back and asked if she wanted to dance some more, she smiled and went with him.

I can't believe she still likes him, knowing he's the kind of person who would prank a girl just because she's an easy target.

I can't believe she didn't even stop dancing long enough to give me a good-luck hug before I left with the band.

This is seriously the worst night ever.

"Genevieve?" calls a voice over the noise of the bathroom, and for a second I perk up. Maybe Syd is here to find me after all. But then the voice says my name again, and I realize it's Mariah. She sounds a little frantic. I really need to pull myself together and help her like I said I would.

I do one last check-in with my stomach, and it seems like my three bites of food are going to stay put. So I stand, brush off the knees of my tights, and open the stall door.

"*There* you are!" Mariah rushes over and grabs my arm. "I've been looking everywhere for you. I need to go over the backup part with you! We only have twenty minutes!"

Only twenty minutes. My stomach flips again, and I almost spin around and shut myself back in the stall. But Mariah's got a pretty firm grip on me.

"Sorry," I say. "Let me wash my hands first."

I squeeze between a couple of girls and glance at my reflection in the mirror as I pump the last remnants of watery soap out of the dispenser. I look clammy and miserable, which makes me wish I hadn't checked. I try three different sinks before I find a sensor that responds to my waving hands, and then the water blasts out so hard I have to leap out of the way before it splashes all over my skirt. I pat my cheeks with cold water carefully so I don't ruin what little mascara I managed to put on, and then I follow Mariah out of the bathroom.

Her legs aren't any longer than mine, but she walks toward the chorus room so quickly I practically have to jog to keep up. "Okay, so the beginning starts quiet, right? I just go *ooooooh* while you sing the first few lines, and then I go up on the harmony for 'standing on my own two feet,' right? And then is it '*I* won't let them get *me* down' or '*We* won't let them get *us* down'?"

She's talking so fast it's making me dizzy. Or maybe I'm dizzy because I'm nervous, like Abby's mom at her grandmother's funeral. Or maybe it's because I've hardly eaten anything. There's a granola bar in my locker, but if I eat it to help with the dizziness, I probably will throw up after all.

"*Genevieve!*" Mariah waves a hand in front of my face, and I flinch. "Sorry! I didn't mean to yell. But are you even listening to me?"

"I'm listening," I say. Mariah can be so bossy sometimes. "It's 'We won't let them get us down.' Do you want to sing through the whole thing with me, and I can tell you if you're doing any of it wrong?"

"Yeah, okay," Mariah says. She reaches for the door of the chorus room, but then there's a burst of laughter and shouting from inside, and she drops her hand. "Ugh, they're being superloud. Let's just do it out here."

I nod, clear my throat, tap my foot to set the tempo, and start singing the first verse of "Hear Us Roar." I've practiced this song a billion times alone in my bedroom, and the lyrics come to me without even thinking. But my voice sounds wrong, flat and faraway, like my head is wrapped in a bunch of blankets. I try to correct it, but I don't seem to have any control. Mariah isn't looking at me weird or anything, so it must not sound as strange as I think. Of course, that's almost worse, knowing the problem is *inside my brain.*

I try to ignore it and help Mariah fix the few things she's doing wrong with the backup part. Unfortunately, it's pretty hard to concentrate when I keep imagining what will happen if I get up onstage and suddenly can't control my voice at all. What if I go temporarily deaf out of panic? Is that even possible?

Somehow, we get all the way through "Hear Us Roar." When we finish, someone says, "That sounded good," and I spin around to find Tess in the doorway of the chorus room, scrolling through something on her phone. I didn't even hear her come out; she must've told Faith and Claudia to be quiet so she could listen.

"Really?" Mariah and I ask at the same time. Then we both laugh, and the pressure in my chest eases a little.

"Yeah, really," Tess says, straight to Mariah. "If it sounded bad, you know I'd tell you." I wish she'd say something reassuring to me, too, but Tess doesn't hand out compliments unless you really deserve them.

Tess looks back down at her screen. "Hey, Genevieve, you're friends with Sydney, right?"

"Me? Yeah." I reach up and touch the music-note necklace, the only proof I have from tonight that we actually *are* friends.

"Are she and Kevin actually a *thing*? He's so basic. Did you hear what he did to Ellie? What a creep."

"What? No, they're not . . . I mean, Syd was dancing with him earlier, but that's it."

"Then what's this about?" Tess holds up her screen so I can see Ilana's latest Instagram post. It's a picture of Syd and Kevin on the dance floor, and even though it was taken from far away, it's still pretty obvious that they're kissing.

The caption reads, *OTP!!!!!!!* 💋 💋 💋 💋 💋 It already has forty-three likes and seventeen comments.

I fumble in my pocket for my own phone. I haven't felt it buzz all night, but if Syd couldn't find me in person, she definitely would've texted to tell me she'd had her very first kiss. There are probably, like, eighteen lines of hearts and exclamation points waiting on my screen; she gets kind of emoji-crazy when she's superexcited. When her family got their dog, she literally sent me *two hundred* dog emojis in a row. And a dog isn't even as big of a deal as this.

I hit the home button.

I have no new messages.

"I . . . um . . ." I stammer, but I can't get any more words out, even though Tess and Mariah are both staring at me with raised eyebrows. The hallway is overheated, but I shiver a little.

Tess looks back down at her phone, then back up at me. "What? Is there a problem? I mean, besides Kevin being King of the Jerks. I think he's even worse than Leif."

The problem is that sadness and betrayal and terror and shame are piling up inside me, and they're taking up so much space that I'm afraid they'll block off my airway entirely. But it's not like I can say that to Tess. She doesn't understand that not everyone is strong and confident like she is, and she's not very tolerant of weakness. She once ripped a book right out of Sadie Rosenberg's hands in English class and took over reading aloud because Sadie kept stumbling over big words.

"Nothing," I choke, because I can't handle her being mad at me on top of everything else. "I'm fine."

"You look kind of weird," Mariah says. "Do you have a headache or something? I have Tylenol in here." She opens her small purse and looks through it. "Or do you want a cough drop? Gum? A Band-Aid? Or—"

"Why do you have all that stuff in there?" asks Tess. "You're like my mom."

Mariah shrugs. "I like to be prepared."

"I'm fine," I say again.

Ms. Huff comes out of the gym and strides down the hall-way toward us, carrying a Hula-Hoop. "You ladies good to go?" she calls. "We'll be ready for you onstage in a few minutes!"

"Yeah, be right there!" Tess shouts back, and then she turns to us. "Come on. Preshow ritual. I'll lead since Carmen's not here."

She herds us into the chorus room, and Claudia and Faith stand up and hold out their arms like we're going to have a group hug. I follow Tess over to them, and they pull Mariah and me into a tight huddle. Faith's arm clamps around my waist on one side, Mariah's on the other, and even though we're in a wide-open room, I start to feel trapped and claustrophobic. I have no idea what's about to happen; I've only been in the band for one other performance, and they must've done this part before I got there.

"Foot in the middle," Tess says. Everyone else is already touching toes in the center of the circle, so I extend my green-sneakered foot. It looks childish next to the other girls' boots and high heels.

Tess counts off, and the girls start chanting.

Feet . . . to . . . feet! We've got that beat, can't stop that beat!
Hip . . . to . . . hip! We're tougher than a battleship!
Back . . . to . . . back! We're serious as a heart attack!
Head . . . to . . . head! We'll make music till we're dead!
Talented and unafraid!
Who are we? WE'RE HEART GRENADE!

There are full-body movements that go along with the chant, but I don't know any of them, so I concentrate on staying on my feet as the other girls fling me back and forth like a rag doll. It makes me feel nauseated all over again. Mariah doesn't know what's going on either, but it doesn't seem to bother her. She just bounces up and down to the beat of the chant and bops her head like she's totally a part of things already.

I don't think I've ever stood so close to a group of people and felt so far away from them at the same time.

Everyone cheers when the chant ends, and then they pull apart. Faith slings her bass over her shoulder, Claudia grabs her guitar, and Tess takes her drumsticks out of her boot. They all push into the hall and head for the gym, toward our television debut.

Mariah holds the door for me. "Ready?" she asks.

I've never been less ready for anything in my entire life.

"Yes," I say.

RYAN { 9:58 P.M. }

TONIGHT IS TURNING OUT TO BE A TOTAL waste. If not for Mariah, I'd probably be home in front of the TV, watching anything but this. Instead, here I stand with a bunch of guys from Social Studies, listening to them make fun of the way everyone else dances. Leif is one of those guys.

They all seem to find it funny that Leif was hiding first behind a plant and then behind Chris, like a scared little kid. I would give him a hard time about it too, but what would be the point? They're being big enough jerks for all of us. I also feel like I need to stick close to Leif tonight so I can keep him away from Mariah. Since my usual guy friends opted to stay home instead of coming to the dance tonight, this is the group I'm stuck with.

So I settle in with them. Maybe their jerky guy-dom will rub off on me. Leif obviously has *something* that girls like. After a few minutes of watching them make mean jokes about people and laugh obnoxiously, I decide that maybe *that's* what I'm missing. Maybe I need to be a jerk in order for Mariah to see me as more than a friend.

A new day. A new Ryan.

I smile to myself and watch the fun. There are a bunch of kids yanking our streamers down, but I don't stop them. Saving Mariah's decorations is something the old Ryan would do. The new Ryan doesn't do a thing. Leif gives me a look—he knows that Mariah and I are on the decoration committee—but when I don't say anything, he joins the others in ripping down streamers as well.

"Isn't the band about to go on?" Chris asks Leif after a while. "Maybe you should go find your *girlfriend.*"

"Which one?" I ask, feeling like someone punched me in the gut. Did he just call Mariah Leif's girlfriend? Or was he talking about Tess?

All the guys burst into laughter, and Chris even punches

Leif playfully in the arm. Leif's cheeks have a light pink tinge. He's . . . embarrassed?

"It's okay, dude, just hide behind the plant over there," Leif's friend Shawn says. "We'll cover for you if Tess comes back."

That brings another round of laughs. I laugh along with them, taking mental notes on how to be a jerk. They snort and punch one another and hunch their shoulders like they're ready to fight. All along, Leif just keeps smiling, not a care in the world.

"Here comes Mariah," one of the guys says, reminding me why I'm trying to be a jerk in the first place. My heart skips a beat, but that's okay. I can still like Mariah. I just have to be chill about it.

By the time Mariah makes her way over to us, Leif has vanished. I don't even know where. Maybe he found something else to hide behind.

Mariah has a huge smile on her face. I haven't seen her this happy since . . . ever. Too bad I'm not the reason for her happiness.

Play it cool, man.

"I have to tell you something!" she gushes as she comes to a stop in front of me. "You won't believe it!"

"Hmph," I say, trying to sound bored.

She motions for me to follow her as she steps off to the side. I decide to go; otherwise she'll just be standing by herself and it'll be awkward.

"I'm an official member of Heart Grenade!" she squeals. "Well, just a backup singer and just for tonight, but still . . . Tess invited me. Can you believe it? Not that we're BFFs or anything."

Wow. Okay. So Mariah and Tess have suddenly ended their major war? All those years of listening to Mariah freak out over Tess—not to mention all the stuff that happened tonight—and one fifteen-minute conversation fixes everything?

Girls are weird.

She stays silent, and I realize she's looking to me for a reaction. What would a jerk do? I have no idea. All I *want* to do is let her know I'm excited for her. This being-a-jerk thing is supertough.

I try to imagine what Leif would do. Probably say *That's great* in a distracted voice and turn back to his friends. Or go hide behind a plant.

"Whatever," I say with the most disinterested expression I can manage. I focus on the area behind her as if I'm looking for a better conversation.

"What's wrong? Are you mad at me?" Mariah asks.

The sad expression on her face makes me feel a little sick. It looks like she might have tears welling in her eyes. I don't want to hurt her. I *never* want to hurt her.

But I won't give in; if I do that, I'll just go back to being the guy whose shoulder she cries on. The one who will never be more than just a friend.

I can't be that guy anymore.

"Nope," I say, still without looking at her. I try to ignore the guilt weighing on me.

Tess is across the gym, standing on tiptoe, looking around. It's just the break I need.

"I think they're waiting for you," I say. And just for good measure, I roll my eyes.

I turn my back to her and try to push back into the group I'd been hanging with before. Only problem? They've closed up their circle and it's kind of awkward getting back in.

"Hey, guys!" I call out, squeezing through until I'm standing between Chris and some dude from my science class. "So Heart Grenade's about to go on."

They all glance at me, and then Chris continues whatever he'd been saying when I spoke up. I frown.

"There he is!" someone yells, and I turn to see Leif behind me. He's dancing with Abby.

"Okay, guys, over here!" another voice calls.

I turn around just in time to see—who else?—that yearbook photographer. His attention isn't on me, though. Maybe I can just creep away without anyone noticing.

"No, you, too," the photographer guy yells as I take what I think is a very subtle step backward. So much for sneaking away.

"Uh, no thanks," I say, realizing that jerks probably wouldn't even say thanks. They'd just say something like *No, man* in a gruff voice and walk off. Nobody stops a jerk from doing what he wants. I have to keep practicing my jerkiness to make sure I have it down when Mariah's around.

"Okay, everyone," Vice Principal Stanwick says through a microphone onstage, cutting into all the chitchat. It takes a minute or two, but eventually the roar dies down. "Heart Grenade is going on in a couple of minutes."

Cheers all around. Mr. Stanwick holds his hand up to silence everyone.

"Just a reminder that we're on live TV," he says. "Your parents will be watching, along with everyone else. Let's show them what a great student body Lynnfield Middle School has.

The DJ is going to play one more song, and then when I give the signal, everyone move toward the stage so we can get a shot with a crowd in front of it."

I move farther away from the group of guys. I have no idea where I'm going. Even if I plan to continue acting like a jerk, I do want to see Heart Grenade perform. I just don't want Mariah to know I'm watching.

The bleachers. They're partly dark, and nobody's really paying attention to the few people scattered over there. I don't make eye contact with anyone as I walk over.

I'm settled on the bleachers when I realize the chaperones are hanging out just a few rows above me. That includes my mom, who spots me right away and clomps over.

"How's it goin'?" she asks, trying for a casual voice but sounding high-pitched and uncomfortable instead.

"Fine. Just resting for a minute."

I don't want to get into everything that's happened with Mariah. I usually don't discuss personal business with my mom. Honestly, I don't even want to be making small talk with her, but she's my *mom*. At least nobody's paying attention to us right now anyway.

"You know what you should do?" she asks.

She's scanning the dance floor. People are making a half-hearted attempt to dance while waiting for the band. They're mostly bouncing up and down a little while they talk.

"Ask a girl to dance," she says. "Any girl. I think that might help with your problem."

My mom thinks I have a problem. No, scratch that; my mom *knows* I have a problem. Moms have that weird psychic ability. And since she's aware of my crush on Mariah, it likely didn't take much for her to figure out what that problem is.

I look over and see Leif still dancing with Abby. They seem to be all flirty, and I know if Mariah sees them she will be furious. So will Tess, probably.

My mom is right. I should be talking to another girl . . . maybe even dancing with one. That way, when the band goes on, Mariah will see me out here with someone else. Maybe she'll finally be interested . . . or even jealous.

I search the gym for someone who might possibly dance with me. My eyes come to rest on a girl from Advanced Algebra named Amanda. She seems nice—the kind of girl who won't laugh in my face.

Now is the time to do something besides wait for Mariah. Now is the time for me to get out there.

RYAN

My heart races as I head toward the dance floor. I'm not sure what makes me more nervous—the idea of asking someone to dance or the thought of Mariah catching us out here. I make my way toward her, trying my best to get past my nerves, and prepare to ask a girl to dance for the first time ever.

ASHLYN { 10:02 P.M. }

I DON'T KNOW HOW IT'S POSSIBLE FOR sixteen blisters to form in the span of walking across one soccer field and one tennis court in damp suede boots, but my heels are as raw as the skin on the back of my neck (hey, thanks, pricker bush!) when we finally reach the back door of the gym. But it will all be worth it because WE ARE HERE! I tug hard on the handle.

Of course it's locked.

So much for sneaking in and beautifying myself in the locker room before showing my face to any of my classmates.

If it weren't for my soggy butt and my seventeen blisters

(seriously, I think they're multiplying by the second), I might even consider just turning around and going back to the Terzettis', because what's even the point of sneaking into a dance when you won't be able to fully enjoy it on account of the twigs in your hair and the chipped edges on your manicure and feet that hurt worse than when you wax between your eyebrows?

But you know what? If I can't be happy tonight, then Ellie *definitely* shouldn't be, since this whole situation is entirely her fault to begin with. It might even be worth risking a few unflattering shots on Instagram just to march in there and toss Kevin aside and dump the Brats on her, even if I don't get to have the full dance experience myself.

"What are we doing?" whines Charity. "Aren't we going around to the main door?"

"Yeah. I'm cold," Hope chimes in.

"You're cold? *You're* cold? I'm the one who had my cheeks on ice in a frigid creek tonight—and I don't mean the cheeks on my face, either!"

They crack up.

I really can't wait to be rid of these two.

I grab their arms and hobble-march us around the side of the building to the front entrance. Ugh, and now my wet socks are all bunched up in my boots. There's a reason I don't do the outdoors!

In the roundabout driveway of the courtyard is a black van with KACT-TV on the side and all kinds of weird satellite dishes on its roof. EEK! I totally forgot about the live broadcast thing! They'd better have the lights dimmed inside, because showing up on Instagram is one thing; looking like this on TV is a whole other matter. I have big plans for my television debut, and those include runway appearances on *Model Marathon* and/or guest judging gigs on *Superstar!* This . . . does not even come close to hitting the list.

"Daddy's truck!" Hope breaks free and races across the courtyard to the propped-open doors leading to the gym.

"What is she talking about?" I ask, tightening my grip on Charity. She slips clear of me and runs off after her sister, turning to yell back, "Our dad works for the TV station!"

Um. What?

What? What? *WHAT?*

Mrs. Terzetti did say her husband had to work tonight, but why wouldn't she have told me he was working *at MY dance?*

Further note: Why wouldn't she have told me her husband was "in the biz," as they say? I would have been a teensy tiny bit more invested in all this babysitting stuff if I'd known there were Hollywood-style perks to be had! Maybe it's not too late. It's entirely possible Mr. Terzetti was just waiting for a good excuse to replace his lawn mower, right? This changes everything!

I break into a run myself (hello, blisters eighteen, nineteen, and twenty).

"Brats! I—I mean, adorable, sweet girls! Wait! You can't . . ."

JADE { 10:03 P.M. }

It's go time. ☺

GENEVIEVE { 10:03 P.M. }

IT'S GO TIME.

My body is with the rest of the band, huddled behind the curtain, waiting for Ms. Huff's cue to go out onstage. But I don't even feel like I'm inside of it anymore. I certainly don't have any control over it. A rushing sound fills my head, like I'm holding an enormous seashell over each ear. My breathing is ragged and shallow, and I can barely feel my legs. I reach out for something to steady myself, but all the other girls are behind me, and there's nothing to grab on to.

Someone shakes my shoulder hard, and I come back to

myself enough to notice that Ms. Huff is frantically waving us forward.

"Genevieve!" Tess hisses behind me. *"Go!"*

Instinct takes over, and suddenly my feet are moving me up the wooden steps and through the break in the curtain. Everyone starts screaming as soon as they see us, and my instinct is to curl up in a ball on the floor as the noise breaks over me like a wave. But I remember the instructions the camera guy gave us, and I force myself to squint into the blazing lights and find the X of hot pink tape on the floor where I'm supposed to stand.

She got up onstage and totally forgot all the words to her song, says Shanti's voice inside my head. *It was like someone erased her brain.*

My little brother threw up during his school play.

My mom always gets really dizzy when she's nervous.

I'm pretty sure I'm not breathing at all, and sparks wink to life in my peripheral vision.

I make myself look past the glare of the lights, past the staring, alien eyes of the cameras, and into the front row of kids, where Sydney said she'd be. Even though she hasn't been the greatest friend tonight, seeing her familiar smile will still make me feel better. Everyone's cheering and reaching out toward the stage like they're at a real concert, but Sydney's not there. I look one more row back, and one more, and one more, but I can't find her anywhere.

The video guy starts counting down on his fingers, and then he points at the vice principal, who is standing on the floor in front of the stage. Mr. Stanwick's voice sounds like it's underwater as he says, "Live from Lynnfield Middle School, I give you Heart Grenade, making their television debut!"

Vaguely, from miles behind me, I hear Tess shout, "One! Two! One, two, three, four!"

The band launches into the first riff of "Hear Us Roar," but even through the blasting amplifiers, Faith's bass sounds far away. Everything is moving too fast and too slowly at the same time.

Three bars left. Then two. Then one. And there's my cue.

I open my mouth.

Nothing comes out.

Tess and Faith falter for a minute, and then they circle back and start playing the intro again. I know everyone's waiting for me, counting on me. The band. The audience. The camera guy. Dad and Papa, sitting on the couch back home. My choir director, who definitely won't want me to sing a solo anymore after she sees this. I'm letting them all down.

I'm sorry, I think to everyone. *I'm so sorry.*

My cue comes around again, and I try harder to join in this time. I really do. But there's an iron band around my lungs, and my vocal cords don't seem to exist at all anymore, and the sparks are dancing across my entire field of vision now.

I pray for a tornado or a tidal wave to hit the gym. Or for an earthquake to open up a giant rift in the middle of the floor. Or for the ceiling to collapse. Not in a way that would hurt anyone. I just need something, anything, to make all of this stop so I can pull myself together.

And that's when all the lights go out.

GENEVIEVE

Did I just make that happen . . . WITH MY MIND?

ELLIE

Really? I honestly didn't think this night could get any darker.

RYAN

Wow. Just wow. I'm standing next to this sweet, cute girl, and all I can do is stare at the dark blob I know is Mariah. I can't even see her anymore, but I can't look away.

ASHLYN

Brats? Brats! Oh God, I hate the dark! Oww! Hey! Who just pulled my hair? Do you even *know* who you're messing with?

TESS

If the power doesn't come back on right this second, I am going to murder the electric company for messing up our big break! *Someone* is going to answer for this.

CARMEN

Noooooooooooooooooooo! What happened to the webpage? Why is it black? Did Heart Grenade just break the Internet!?!

JADE

Success! On to phase three!

JADE { **10:06 P.M.** }

I'M BACK IN THE LOCKER ROOM. *AGAIN.* I couldn't risk grabbing the refills of soap until I was sure no one would see me with them. According to my calculations, I have about three minutes to get the supplies and run them to the gym, where my fumbling accomplice is *supposed* to be waiting to help me.

As absentminded as he is, he's actually a genius. No really, he is. And apparently he pays close attention to what his dad does—#ElectricianFTW. Not only did he manage to figure out how to cut the power (I didn't even ask—too complicated for me), he also came up with a plan to delay the generator (even more complicated, so I hear).

That wooden platform will be more like a slippery ice rink than a stage once I'm done with it. But the delay will only last so long, so if I don't hurry, the generator *will* kick the lights back on and it'll be too late to sneak in there unnoticed.

I set the timer on my phone and push the little icon to turn on the flashlight app. I scan the rows of lockers to find the right one. Number forty-three, there you are. I open it up and reach my hand in to grab the backpack, but I can't find it. I point the beam of light into the locker. It's empty.

"What? Where is it?" I say out loud. I check my phone. A little over two minutes left. Grrr.

"Looking for this?"

I whip my flashlight in the direction of the voice. A girl in an old-fashioned dress holds up the backpack full of the soap refills that I really, really need right now.

"Who are *you*?" I ask, as if it matters. "That's my stuff." I reach for the bag, but Little Miss Old-Fashioned pulls it away.

"I'm the girl who's not going to let you get away with this despicable plan of yours," she says, her voice a little shaky. She points at the fluorescent bulbs on the ceiling. "And I'm assuming the lights were 'phase two'?"

I take a step forward. "Oh honey, you did not just do air quotes like phase two wasn't a brilliant plan."

"I sure did." She's obviously trying to sound tough, but her wet-noodle posture and lip-biting give her away. She clutches the bag, and one of the soap refills hangs out the unzipped side, about to take a nosedive onto the tile floor.

"You seriously think you can stop me?" I laugh and point the beam of light directly into her face. She closes her eyes briefly, but not long enough to give me the opening I need to snatch the supplies back.

Little Miss Old-Fashioned grips the bag tighter. "I'm sorry," she says. "But I can't let you do this."

"Here's the thing." She stiffens when I take another step toward her. "You might be the one with the supplies I need, but I'm the one with the flashlight."

I push the off icon, making the locker room pitch-black again, and feel for my pocket to slip the phone back in. I reach forward to grab the backpack. I literally do not have time for this wannabe superhero and her tough-girl act. I manage to grip part of the bag, but the girl pulls back. The sound of the zipper is pretty clear as the front of the backpack separates from the back and I lose my balance. When the soap refills clunk to the floor, we both dive for them and smack shoulders as we land hard. There's a loud *POP*, and the soap oozes beneath us, my hand covered in it. I fumble around and grab as many of the refills as I can. I manage to push myself back up despite my shoe sliding out from under me a couple of times.

I hurry toward the door, feeling my way along the smooth tile walls as my feet slide side to side like I'm ice-skating. One of the refills has sprouted a leak, and the soap runs in a steady stream down my arm. If I'm going to have any chance at all of pulling this off, I have to get to that stage at lightning speed.

"You won't get away with this," yells the girl, her voice coming closer. And before I can take another step, she's tugging at my leg, the soap on her hands soaking through my tights.

"Get off of me!" I hiss, shaking my leg to try to lose her. But Little Miss is determined, I'll give her that. She's gripping on tightly as she slithers across the floor, keeping pace with me. As I reach for the door, she pushes herself up and grabs for the soap. I have to use both arms to ward her off.

"I'm sorry," she says. "But I am officially foiling your plan."

"No, you're not," I say, tugging at the refills. If this nitwit doesn't let go, the whole night will be for nothing!

"Yes. I. AM!" she says even more forcefully as she tugs right back, sending soap flying everywhere.

And when the lights surge back on, brightening the whole room and giving away who I am, I have no choice but to agree.

Well, sort of.

"Give me one sec," I say to the girl, who shoots me a look that says she most certainly will not. But I manage to grab my phone and get a message off anyway.

Stuck in locker room. Let phase 4 loose!

ELLIE { **10:09 P.M.** }

I SQUINT, ADJUSTING MY EYES TO THE light. The girl actually looks a little afraid, which almost makes me laugh. I don't think anyone's ever been scared of me before. I use it to my advantage, though, and glare at her, doing my best Ashlyn impression. It must work, because after a few seconds, she holds her hands up.

"Fine. I surrender."

"Really?" I look at her sideways.

"Yes, really," she says. "My supplies are ruined and the lights are back on."

"Well. I'm glad to see you changed your mind." I cross my arms in front of my chest.

"I didn't change my mind," she says. "There's just no point now." The girl sinks down on the bench. "Besides, it probably wouldn't have worked anyway. My accomplice isn't all that skilled in sabotage." Her voice isn't confident anymore, and I actually feel sorry for her. I know what it's like to want something so much that you can't think straight. That's the entire reason I'm here tonight, after all.

"This was *supposed* to be the best night ever. All my hard work would have paid off when I evened the score with Heart Grenade. But instead the whole thing is a bust," she says. "You're right, it was a despicable plan."

There's soap all over the locker room floor. I'm afraid to move my foot even one inch for fear of slipping and falling on my head. Not to mention ruining my dress even more than it already is.

My dress. My mom's dress. What would she think of all this? I imagine her standing next to me, and what I see is . . . laughter. She's laughing! In my mind she's telling me that she's proud of me. That I did the right thing. That the dress can be fixed. That maybe this night can be fixed.

"Oh, I don't know," I say. "It was a good plan."

Her face brightens a little. "You think so?"

"Yes, I do. Evil, but good. It was like something straight out of a thrilling novel." I slide my feet across the soapy floor until I reach the bench and then sit down next to her. "And maybe you would have actually gotten away with it, if I weren't in the right place at the right time."

"Yeah, how did you manage that, anyway?" she asks. "I did a complete scan of the locker room."

"I was in one of the bathroom stalls. When I heard you, I picked my feet up."

The girl grins. "Sneaky."

I shrug.

"I'm Jade," she says.

I hold out my hand. "I'm Ellie."

We sit in silence for a minute, the girl twirling a ring on her finger. She checks her phone and glances at the door as if she's planning her escape.

"Can I ask you something?" I say.

"Sure," Jade answers.

"Why did you want to sabotage the band?"

She sighs. "To get justice."

"Justice?" I ask.

"My band was up against Heart Grenade in the Battle of the Bands and lost. But it was *totally* rigged." She shakes her head. "They had a relative *and* a family friend on the committee. Do you believe that?"

I nod to show her I understand.

"So I came up with this plan. But my lead singer didn't want to help me because it was too extreme." She shrugs. "She's outside *peacefully* protesting the band while I'm in here trying to make things right."

So it was Jade's friend who nearly knocked me over while I was outside waiting for Kevin. Maybe the girl isn't as "peaceful" as Jade thinks.

"What do you play?"

"Huh?" Jade crinkles her nose.

"In the band?"

"Oh." A big grin spreads across her face. "Guitar."

"That's great," I say. "And I can understand why you feel bad. I'm really sorry."

She laughs. "No, you're not. I bet it was fun foiling my plan."

"Well—" I begin.

But her phone beeps, cutting me off.

"Ellie, I need to go take care of something," she says, standing up. "Like, right now. But great chatting with you."

I shake my head. "Fine, but I'm coming with you." When I stand up, Jade looks shocked. "What'd you expect, that I'd let you out with no supervision?" I give her my best Ashlyn smirk, and we make our way across the floor, tiptoeing through the soap-free spots.

As we near the exit, the side door squeaks open and the locker room is filled with echoes of loud . . . quacking?

And then they come into view.

"Jade?" I stare at the ducks, then back at her, and then at the ducks again. "What have you done now?"

She checks her phone again as a line of ducks parades right through the locker room, quacking and stomping their little webbed feet. They're not slipping on the soap; in fact, they look perfectly at home.

A boy with a camera strapped around his neck comes running around the corner. I recognize him as the yearbook photographer.

Jade steps closer to him. "What did you do?" she asks.

"You said 'ducks in locker room,'" he answers, like it's obvious.

Ahh, this must be the accomplice!

"I said STUCK in locker room!!" Jade does not look happy.

Another duck comes waddling around the corner like he's late for the party.

"Oh, shoot. I messed up again, didn't I?" The boy takes a deep breath and pulls out his phone. "Hey, wait, it wasn't me. See?"

Jade and I both lean in to read their text exchange, and he's right, it says "ducks."

Oh, autocorrect.

The chirpy voice of one of the teachers comes over the loud-speaker in a chirpy voice. "Boys and girls, if you were caught outside the gym during the blackout, please make your way back in so we can make sure everyone is accounted for, just in case we have another issue. The power has obviously been restored, and as soon as everything is set, the band will be going on live."

I stare right at Jade as the ducks continue their quacking. "The clock is ticking, Evil Mastermind. You have to make a decision. You can end this now and get these ducks out of here, or you can release them into the gym so they're a major distraction and nobody will care about the band. That was your endgame, right? The way you'd get your revenge?"

She pauses and then nods.

"Well?" I stand firm.

"So, you're *actually* going to let me walk out of here with these ducks and ruin it all for the band?" she asks.

"If that's what you really want." I soften my voice. "But I don't think it is."

"And how do you know what I want?" Jade glares at me. "We just met."

"True," I say. "But I know that you're interested in justice and doing what's fair."

"That's why I'm here." Jade crosses her arms.

"I also know one of the girls in the band. She's the lead singer. She doesn't deserve to have her big moment ruined."

Jade stays focused on me. "And why not?"

"Because she was the only one who was nice to me tonight." The ducks waddle across the locker room floor, oblivious to their importance in our conversation.

"I don't get it," Jade says.

I take a deep breath. "Tonight was absolutely the most humiliating night of my life. This boy who I've had a crush on for years actually asked me to the dance."

"And that's a *bad* thing?" Jade raises her eyebrows. "Sounds pretty great to me."

"It's a bad thing when he only did it as a joke. And the one person who didn't know that was me."

"Ouch," Jade says, her face looking like she just downed a gallon of sour milk.

"Yeah. So when all the other kids were making a joke out of me, Genevieve was the only one who wasn't laughing. She even asked if I was okay."

"Well, she's still part of the cheating band." Jade's tone is a little bit softer now. It's almost as if she's trying to convince herself.

"You don't actually know that the band had anything to do with how the judges voted."

"I told you . . . ," Jade starts, but I hold up my hand.

"Think about it, Jade. Maybe the band members didn't even know who would be judging. I'm just saying that things aren't always what they seem to be."

Jade opens her mouth to say something, but I take this opportunity to keep talking. "Life isn't always fair. Believe me, I know that more than anyone. But you keep going and hope for the best. So Heart Grenade won the contest—"

"Battle of the Bands," Jade says.

"Fine. So they won the Battle of the Bands this time. Your band will win next time."

"And if we don't?" Jade stares right at me.

"Then you keep trying until you do. That's life."

She pushes her lips together and her eyes turn into little slits as the ducks surround us and the accomplice stands there bobbing his head back and forth between us.

"Can I ask you something?" she says.

I nod.

"Don't you want to get revenge on this boy? I mean, it's totally uncool what he did to you."

I pause for a few seconds, but that's all it takes to know revenge wouldn't make me feel any better.

"No," I answer. "Sometimes you just have to do your best to move forward."

"Move forward," Jade repeats.

"Yes."

I wait as we have a mini–staring contest, but her eyes don't give anything away. Have I convinced her, or have I made her even more determined?

"You're tougher than I thought you were, Ellie," she says. "And if you can handle what happened to you like a total champ, I guess I have no excuse." Jade takes a deep breath, lets it out quickly, and turns to the accomplice. "Can you help us get these ducks out of here?"

He shrugs. "Whatever you say, boss."

I bite my lip to hide my smile, and without a word, the three of us do our best to lead the ducks toward their carriers.

But just as Jade reaches for the handle, the door swings open and knocks her right into me. I lose my balance on the slick floor, and before I can stop them, my feet slip out from under me. I fall to the floor, a scream escaping my lips as I do. As Jade slides over to try to help me, she slips too. She winds up next to me on her back, her feet straight up in the air. Jade turns around so that she's on her hands and knees. She struggles to stand, but the soap suds make that impossible. Instead, she flops down on top of me, her elbow just missing my face by an inch. I try to roll away, but her hand is pinning me down by my hair.

The ducks are now going crazy, feathers flying and beaks quacking. Their little webbed feet are scattering in all directions, and instead of helping, Jade's accomplice is taking pictures.

"What the . . ." Ashlyn tears through the door, her hair a tangled mess and her clothes soaking wet. She takes one look at Jade and me, and her face hardens. "WHAT ARE YOU DOING TO MY SISTER?!"

I look around to see who Ashlyn's talking about. Is it possible that the sister she's talking about is *me*?

Ashlyn grabs Jade's arm, but Jade tears it away. "Let go of me!"

"Let go of *her*!" Ashlyn screeches. I've never seen her looking so scary.

"Would you let me explain?" Jade pulls herself up, her feet sliding every which way beneath her. "The door knocked into me, and I knocked into Ellie."

"Is this true?" Ashlyn asks me, her voice hard and on edge.

"Yes," I say. "It was an accident."

A duck waddles between Ashlyn's feet, and she shrieks. "What is going on—"

Just then, the locker room door bursts open again. This time, a bunch of girls rush in. The soapy floor causes them to crash into one another, but they wind up in a huddle and stay on their feet. My stomach sinks when I see their faces; they're the same girls who teased me about Kevin—and they're Ashlyn's friends.

Shanti takes one look at me, the ducks, and the soapy floor and bursts out laughing.

"Omigod, Ashlyn. What's going on?" Ilana's hand flies up

to her mouth. "Does this have something to do with the lights going out?"

"What?" Ashlyn smooths her shirt.

"After the lights went out, everyone started saying it was part of some big prank. And now this!" She does a sweeping gesture with her arm—toward us, the soap, and the ducks. "Ashlyn, did you totally stop them?!"

"Yeah, well . . ." Ashlyn flips her hair.

"It was *you*, wasn't it?" Ilana glares at me. "Did you do this to get back at everyone because of the Kevin thing?"

"What? No—"

But Abby interrupts me like I'm not even there and beams at Ashlyn. "You're, like, a hero."

"It must have been some fight," Shanti says to Ashlyn. "Look at you!"

Ashlyn glances down at her clothes, and then back up at the girls. But she doesn't say a word.

I swallow the lump in my throat. For a second there, it seemed like Ashlyn actually cared about me. She even called me her sister. I never thought she'd view me that way, and for a minute, it felt really nice. I sigh. It seems disappointment is the theme of the evening.

JADE { **10:13 P.M.** }

"ARE YOU KIDDING ME?" I ASK, BECAUSE there is no way these girls are for real. "Ellie, are you seriously going to stand there and—"

"Forget it," she says before I can even finish. "It doesn't matter."

"Of course it matters." I throw my arms up, ready to say more, but Ellie gives me a pitiful, pleading look, and I bite my tongue. There's clearly more to this story.

The gaggle of girls slides over to the one they're calling Ashlyn, and they wrap their arms around her. The ducks are surprisingly quiet during all of this, like they're watching a soap opera (pun intended).

I give Ellie a sideways glance and then turn to Ashlyn. "Well, since *you've* foiled my plan, can you at least help us get these ducks out of here?"

And before Ashlyn can tell me there's no way on earth she'd ever touch a farm animal (because I'm 100 percent sure that's what a girl like her would say), another girl steps closer to one of the ducks.

"What's on their feathers?" she asks. "1 . . . 2 . . . 3 . . . 5 . . . 6 . . . 7."

I exchange looks with my accomplice and lift my chin slightly toward the girls. I'm pretty sure he catches on to my telepathic message—*Let's encourage the ducks to teach these girls a lesson.*

He nods and pulls a handful of seeds out of his pocket. "I'll get the ducks outside," he says, walking toward the door. He goes to throw the seeds, but trips, and the seeds go flying— right by Ashlyn's and one of her minions' feet. The ducks instantly beeline for the food.

"Eww! Get them away!" Ashlyn shouts, waving her hands out in front of her.

One of the girls looks right at the accomplice. "Hey, aren't you that yearbook photographer?"

"Oh, right," he says, "Good idea. This *has* to be in the yearbook. You're Shanti, right?" He grabs the camera that's strapped around his neck and snaps pictures of the girls' horrified faces. I have to say, despite his mishaps, he's growing on me.

Shanti takes a few steps backward as one of the ducks follows her and nips at her shoes. His beak opens and then snaps shut on the end of a thin, sky-blue ribbon tied into a bow on her dress. As the duck pulls, the ribbon slips out of the loops one by one until it's not even attached anymore.

"He's ruining my dress!" Shanti shouts.

My accomplice pushes his lips together, but his smile can't be stopped. Ellie throws a hand over her mouth in what looks like an attempt to hide her own smile.

Not that she'd ever admit it, but I'm pretty sure she's at least a little bit happy to see some karma in action tonight.

And I couldn't agree more.

And then, as if that duck were at the starting line of an Olympic sprint race, he takes off running, and all his ducky friends follow behind him.

"OH, NO!" I shout, slapping my hands to my face. "Your

dress is a disaster. We have to get that duck!" The duck has already disappeared behind the lockers, but the girls just stand there with wide eyes like they have no idea what to do. "I think it was number four. Go get it!" I'm in full drama mode, and I'm pretty sure Ellie is on to me and knows I'm messing with these girls now. But she just smiles, apparently choosing not to deny me a little bit of fun.

"Find number four and get my ribbon back!" Shanti leads the charge, and the others follow, ironically, just like a line of ducks.

And at that moment, as the girls start running around the locker room on their mission, Ellie looks at me with an expression of *Jade, you little devil, you.*

She leans over toward me and whispers, "I'm guessing there *isn't* a number four?"

And I wait for her to get mad. To tell those girls they're on a wild-goose-slash-duck chase. But when I fist-bump her and say, "That one was for you," the biggest smile I've seen tonight spreads across her face.

ASHLYN { 10:15 P.M. }

POSSIBLE SIGNS A ZOMBIE APOCALYPSE IS upon us:

1. I am in public—at a *school dance*—looking like I went dumpster diving after swimming the English Channel.

2. I called Ellie my sister.

3. I CALLED ELLIE MY SISTER!

4. It felt kind of okay.

There are also ducks flapping and quacking everywhere. I shriek and leap onto a bench to avoid both them and my friends giving chase. I'm not sure where ducks figure into a zombie apocalypse; I just know I'm not going to get even grosser slipping around in soap and duck poop to find out.

And as for the sister thing . . .

Okay, so I have no clue where *that* word came from; I just know that I saw Ellie on the floor with some strange girl holding her down and it was like I snapped. I think maybe in a past life I must have been a member of the Royal Guard or something, because my protective instincts are clearly very heightened and I never ever knew it. (FYI, I'm pretty sure I was also Cleopatra in a past life, and I don't know why no one believes me when I say that, even though my obsession with cats and arm bangles makes it sooo obvious.)

"Now one is nibbling on my shoe strap!" Shanti says, from the next aisle over.

Maybe Ellie didn't hear me call her my sister. That's possible, right? She's definitely avoiding eye contact now. She and that attacker girl are too busy giggling over something like they're besties. Are they besties? I really don't know that much about who Ellie hangs with, I guess.

"I'm gonna go . . . get Ms. Huff and . . . tell her what happened," Abby says, reappearing in my row of lockers and stopping. She puts her hands on her knees. While she tries to catch her breath, she says, "Ashlyn, you . . . should . . . stay here. I'll bet she'll want to . . . thank you or . . . give you an award or . . . something."

She holds up a finger and takes a deep breath, exhaling slowly before adding, "Maybe they'll present you with the key to the city or the mayor will declare this date Ashlyn Day. How cool would that be?"

So cool. Obviously, I am fully in favor of Ashlyn Day being a thing. Preferably, it would include a parade. And confetti cannons.

But.

I steal another glance at Ellie, who's now staring at her hands, and my stomach does this weird swoopy thing. Huh? What is happening to me? Am I getting sick? Maybe the creek water had icky bacteria in it or something. Why am I feeling so . . .

Guilty.

So *what* if I get the credit for stopping the Great Soap Slide instead of Ellie? I mean, we're talking about *Ellie*.

Before I can even think about what I'm doing, I shrug at Abby. "Yeah, well, so I guess it was kind of Ellie who foiled things, or whatever."

Abby turns her head to Ellie, her eyes wide.

Oh my God, what did I just do? This is so— Wait! Maybe

the creek didn't have bacteria. Maybe it had a tapeworm that got in under my skin and is crawling around inside my brain right now and making me feel all sisterly and . . . sweet. This sucks.

"Is that true?" Ilana asks, also facing Ellie now with one hand on her hip.

Shanti appears too, with her ribbon in one hand and a single shoe dangling from the other. They seem to have abandoned the duck hunt to the boy with the camera around his neck. From a few rows over I hear him croon, "Here, ducky, ducky, duckies!"

"I—I—" Ellie's staring at me with superwide eyes. (Which, I note, could use a little more mascara, if I'm being honest. Take that, tapeworm.) "I guess so?"

"Oh well, whatever." Ilana shrugs, then turns to Abby and Shanti and says, "Let's go, girls—I've had all I can take of this madness."

Abby squints. "Um, you don't want to, uh, maybe use the mirror first?"

Shanti glances at the ribbon from her dress. "I'm willing to brave the haunted bathroom. Some creaking pipes are way preferable to this . . . quack show!"

She steps forward and slips on the soap, throwing her arms up to catch herself against the wall she slides into. "Argh!" she screams.

They begin to file out, but something occurs to me and I yell after them.

"Hey, wait," I ask. "Where's Sydney? I thought she was hanging with you guys tonight."

Abby darts a glance at Ellie before giggling. "Oh, she's busy . . . with Kevin."

The others laugh too, and I raise my eyebrows. "Still?"

Are they saying he ditched his actual date to hang out with Syd? Wait, what?!? Normal Ashlyn would probably be laughing here too, but instead I glance at Ellie. She's studying the floor like she's counting the tiles or something, and it does NOT help the swooping situation in my belly.

"Coming, Ash?" Abby asks.

"Yeah, I'll be there in a sec." I point to my hair. "I'm gonna use the mirror in here. That haunted bathroom creeps me out."

Shanti throws one last evil look toward the back of the locker room, where the quack noises are quieting. "I'm never, ever forwarding another cute duck video from YouTube. Those things are . . . monsters!"

The girls slam out of the room and it's quiet for a second, until a lone *pip!* sounds.

"I guess I'd better help him get them out the side door," the attacky girl says. She stands and brushes her hands on her legs before telling Ellie, "It was really nice meeting you."

Ellie gives the girl a small smile and resumes twisting her hands in her lap. I can't believe she's made friends with this girl instead of insisting we turn the evildoer in for master scheming crimes, but I kind of can't be bothered with it. I have to focus on me right now—specifically, solving the mystery of what is happening to my insides.

Neither of us speaks as we listen to the door in the back of the locker room open. There's some muffled talking between the girl and the yearbook kid, a final shuffling, and then all is quiet. I sigh and step down from the bench I've been standing on, instead plopping next to Ellie on hers.

I should be addressing the burrs-and-twigs-in-hair situation, but my blisters need a minibreak. "So what's up with that whole Sydney thing? How come she's hanging out with *your* Kevin?"

Oh, whoa. I mean, not *her* Kevin, because really he's way more my friend than hers, and before tonight even the thought of them in the same room was kind of—well, I'll just say it, comical—but he did ask her to the dance, so, I mean . . .

Ellie snort-laughs, which is so not something Ellie ever does. Was there something in the punch at this dance or what?

"He's certainly not *my Kevin*. The entire date was an enormous fraud. As it turns out, he only asked me as a joke."

She bites her lip and blinks a few times fast, like I do when I'm trying to settle fake eyelashes into place. But since Ellie would never wear false lashes, it's almost like she's trying to hold back tears or something.

Immediately, my gut does that backflipping thing again.

I mean, on the one hand, Ellie is exactly the perfect target for a prank like this, and I get why he picked her.

But *he* doesn't have to see her camped out in here like she's planning to move in and pull a Moaning Myrtle for the rest of time. And he's not the one who knows how long Ellie spent getting ready or how she wore her mom's dress just for him. Not to mention my grandmother's headband! My *halmoni* might have been a tiny Korean woman who'd only come up to Kevin's shoulder, but she would whoop his butt if she were here right now.

Wait, I'm a tiny Korean girl. Maybe *I* can whoop his butt. Because he can't just get away with doing this to her! The other thing my *halmoni* would say is, "Family first," and as much as I can't believe I'm going to say this, it kind of feels like Ellie is part of mine now.

"This is so not acceptable. We are gonna take immediate and irrevocable action on this!" I pause when I catch her expression. "Why are you *smiling*? We need to make him pay for what he's done to you!"

Ellie glances at me. "I'm smiling because you said 'we' and also because you know the word 'irrevocable.'"

I roll my eyes. "Of course I do. I'm not a total puffhead, you know."

"I know. You're more like Tralalia on *Secret Lives of Celebrity Sisters*. There was this time she almost got arrested for swimming in the fountain at the mall and she got out of a ticket by quoting a really obscure bylaw in the Beverly Hills city code, which was quite unexpected."

My jaw drops to the floor. "You did not just reference *SLCS*!"

Ellie shrugs. "It's one of my guilty pleasures."

"Nooooooo way!" She can't be for real right now. That is the very last thing I would have expected her to say. I thought her favorite TV show would be more like *World's Boringest Skills, Such as How to Churn Butter Like the Colonists Did* or something.

It's not even possible that she's a *true* fan of something as trendy as *SLCS*. I'll bet she just wandered by the TV and caught that one part of one episode. There's an easy way to catch her in a lie here. "Which girl is your favorite?"

She doesn't miss a beat. "Well, I suppose Serenity Loveyish, because she's very overshadowed by the other two and she's actually quite sweet."

She totally watches it!

"No. Way. She's my fave too!" I can't help but let out a tiny squeal, which echoes around the empty locker room. Omigosh, I'm talking about S. Lovey with *Ellie*.

"I especially like how they're so different, but they're sisters, so they make it work," she says.

I feel like she's trying to send me some kind of message. Her smile is kind of, I don't know, meaningful or expectant or something. But it's sort of pretty, too. I lean back a little more and fully take in her appearance.

Oh. Oh, *yikes*.

"You know, you're kind of a mess. You look like you went

ten rounds with Mr. Clean," I say, running my eyes up and down her soapy dress.

Ellie's eyes go wide again, but then she blinks and raises her eyebrows and says, "Yes, well, you should talk. You look like you crawled out of a sewage pipe."

Um, what? She did NOT just— Although I happen to catch sight of our reflections in the mirror across from us, and I'm all bunched shirt and scratched arms and twiggy hair and she's all soapy and disheveled, and yeah, she's right. We're both megatragic at the moment.

Then she starts laughing and then *I* start laughing and then we're laughing *together*.

And there are no zombies or apocalypses anywhere in sight. So. Weird.

When we can breathe normally again, I glance at her. "I'm pretty sure it was Khloe Kardashian who once said, 'When it comes to guys, the best revenge is looking good.' I say we show Kevin exactly what he's missing out on. When he comes begging for you to date him for real, we can laugh right in his squashed-looking face!"

Ellie's expression can only be described as *Have you gone round the bend, babycakes?* (which of course she'd probably say as *Excuse me, but have you misplaced a few brain cells?*), but I just smile and shrug.

What she actually says is: "I don't believe in revenge, but I *am* all about karma. Only, how would I achieve that while looking like this?"

"First of all, it sucks what happened to your mom's dress, but at least it's only soap, which means it should totally wash out. So that's good. Second of all, you're in luck because *I* have extra clothes in my locker and I'll bet they'd fit you, if you want. The whole reason I'm in here in the first place is 'cause I was coming to grab them."

"But then what about you? What'll you change into?"

I shrug. "I'm good. I mean, my first choice was to 'refabulous' myself, but when it comes down to it, the best part of being popular is if you act like you're doing something on purpose, no one questions it. Even better, they copy it. Maybe I can start a new "sewage pipe" fashion movement. Anyway, it'll be completely worth it to watch Kevin squirm worse than a baby hamster in a Halloween costume when he sees you looking *a-d-o-r-a-b-l-e* as we march straight past him and out the door. I'll call my mom to see how soon she can get here, so we don't have to hang around for the last forty-five minutes.

Oh, crud. My phone! Well, whatever. We'll get you fixed up, then we'll find one to borrow. Now, my threads are totally way more trendy than you're used to, but it's zero problem for me to show you how to wear them the right way."

I catch Ellie rolling her eyes. "What? What'd I say?" I ask.

She smiles and shakes her head. "Nothing. That would be really lovely."

Lovely? Ugh. Who even says that in this century? She's so superlucky to have me as a sister, because not many other people would have the stamina to take on a project as big as Ellie is going to be. Although she does have a decent head start with her choice in TV shows, so maybe there's hope for my soon-to-be sister after all.

"Okay, come on, Ells." I stand and hold out my hand, and she lets me yank her up. We link arms to keep each other from slipping on any duck droppings or soap as we make our way to my locker and I spin the combo lock. I'm just handing her a supercute purple cami from inside when she asks, "I still can't figure out what you're doing here. Did the Terzettis come home early? Did they drop you off here instead of at our house, because it— Oh! What is it? Why did your eyes get all big like that?"

"Um . . . because . . . no reason. Yup. Nope, it's . . . nothing at all! Hey, uh, I'll be right back. One sec, okay?"

I run from the aisle and use my momentum to slide across the soapy floor the whole way to the door, both arms out to stop myself when I hit it hard. I yank it open and dash into the gym.

"Brats? BRATS? I DEFINITELY DIDN'T FORGET ALL ABOUT YOU! I'M COMING, YOU GUYS!"

GENEVIEVE { 10:20 P.M. }

"I CANNOT BELIEVE THIS."

The minute Ms. Huff finally finds us all in the chaos and manages to corral us behind the stage, Tess starts pacing back and forth and back and forth across the narrow strip of polished floor. Her hands are buried deep in her hair like she's going to rip it out by the roots. It's making me kind of woozy to watch her. Or maybe I feel weird because of the way the lights are flickering as they slowly, slooowwwly warm back up after the blackout. Then again, I felt pretty awful to begin with, so maybe it has nothing to do with Tess or the lights. I hug my knees to my chest and press my back flat against the wall, trying to disappear so no one will ask me what happened onstage.

"We still get to play," Claudia says. "Ms. Huff said we just have to wait until the next opening in the broadcast, and then they'll—"

Tess keeps talking like Claudia hasn't even said anything. "This is *so important*, and the school can't even be bothered to keep the *lights* on—"

"I don't think it's the school's fault," Mariah says. "Ilana posted something on Instagram about how someone was trying to sabotage the band, and—"

Tess turns on her. "Are you *serious*? Someone hates us enough to *sabotage* us?"

Claudia's mouth drops open. "Who would do something like that?"

"A couple of the boys were making fun of Heart Grenade in PE the other day, but they're probably too lazy to actually sabotage us," Faith says.

"It wasn't them," says Mariah. "Ilana's post says it was a girl."

"If I find out who, I'm going to make her sorry she ever *heard* of Heart Grenade," Tess says. There are basically laser beams shooting out of her eyes.

"It's probably good we get to start over, honestly," Faith says. "That wasn't exactly our best performance."

And then comes the thing I've been fearing most: Tess turns her laser eyes on me.

"Yeah, what happened out there, Genevieve? Did you forget when your cue is? It's drums and bass for eight measures, and then you come in. You had it right in rehearsal yesterday."

I open my mouth to tell her I know when the cue is, but what comes out isn't words. It's this horrible, wet, choked sound. And then, to my horror, I'm suddenly crying in front of the whole band.

Tess's eyes widen. "Oh my God. Are you okay?" She crouches down in front of me, and when Mariah joins her, the ruffles on their identical purple dresses bunch up around their legs in the exact same way. If I weren't completely miserable, it would actually be kind of funny. Mariah offers me a tissue from her bottomless purse, and I take it and blot my eyes.

"Don't do that," says Faith. "Your mascara's getting everywhere."

"Are you sick? Should I get a teacher?" asks Claudia.

I shake my head. It's bad enough that all the girls are seeing me like this; I don't want anyone else coming back here. "No, it's okay. I'm okay."

"You're obviously not," Tess says. "What's the matter? Are you going to be able to sing?"

I expect her to be furious, but when I glance up at her face, she doesn't look angry at all. She looks kind of . . . soft and concerned. And not about the band or our TV broadcast. She looks like she might actually care about *me*, personally.

"I ruined everything. I'm so, so sorry." Saying it out loud triggers a fresh flood of tears.

"You didn't ruin anything," Mariah says. "The jerk who turned the power off ruined everything."

"But I—I got up there, and I—couldn't—" I hiccup and wipe my eyes again, even though I'm probably making my makeup even worse. "My voice, it wouldn't—and I got so scared, and I totally panicked, and—I'm *so* sorry."

"Oh," Tess says, and for some reason, she looks relieved. "It's just stage fright."

There's no "just" about it. Standing up there with spots dancing in front of my eyes and an iron band around my chest and a voice that didn't work was pretty much the worst feeling I've ever had in my entire life. But I nod.

"Well, that's a relief," Tess says. "I thought something was really wrong with you. Why didn't you tell us you were freaking out?"

"I tried to earlier, but you seemed really busy looking for Leif, and then there was the thing with Kate's teeth, and Mariah needed to learn the song, and . . . I don't know. I felt stupid, and it didn't seem important, and I thought . . . I didn't want you all to be mad."

Mariah hands me another Kleenex; she seems to have an endless supply. "Why would anyone be *mad*?"

"Stage fright's totally normal," Tess says. "It happens to everybody."

"Not you guys."

She looks confused. "Of course it happens to us."

"The first time we ever performed together, I was so scared I played an entire song in the wrong key," Claudia tells me. "*A whole song*. It sounded *awful*, but I couldn't do anything about it. It was like my hands weren't even connected to my body." She wiggles her fingers, and her turquoise nail polish sparkles.

Faith laughs. "I kept trying to get her attention, but it was like she was in a trance. Her eyes looked all creepy and glazed over."

"They did not!" Claudia says.

"They did. It was like you were a zombie." Faith makes a slack-jawed face to demonstrate.

Claudia laughs. "Oh man, I'm glad almost nobody was there for that."

"I had a stomachache for two days before our first show," Tess says. "Going up onstage in front of all those people—it's superscary. Especially if you're not used to it."

I know it shouldn't make me feel better to hear about other people being miserable, but it kind of does. Maybe Tess and Faith and Claudia aren't cut out for this more than I am. Maybe they've just had more practice.

"But none of you are freaking out now," I say. "How did you make it stop?"

Tess sits down next to me, and the way her shoulder presses against mine makes me feel more grounded. "It never goes away completely, but the more you do it, the easier it gets," she says. "Deep breathing helps too. I know it sounds stupid, but I swear it works. You breathe in through your nose for three counts, then out through your mouth for five. Try it. In, two, three . . . Out, two, three, four, five . . ."

It does sound kind of silly, but I do what she says, and

suddenly my lungs start to open up again. Air swirls into the very bottom, the part that felt totally cut off before.

"Good," says Tess. "Keep doing that. You're gonna be fine."

"And make sure your knees aren't locked when you're standing onstage," Faith says. "I don't know why, but it keeps you from getting dizzy. I try to bounce a little to the beat. My uncle taught me that. He plays guitar for this band called Neil's Evil Hamster."

I nod and keep breathing. I wish I had asked these girls for advice *before* I got up onstage. It would've been eight billion times more helpful than listening to Abby and Ilana and Shanti babble on about fainting and puking or waiting for Sydney to notice I needed her.

"People say you should picture the audience in their underwear, but I don't get how that's supposed to help," Claudia says. "Seriously, who wants to see that?"

Tess wrinkles her nose. "Ugh, Ms. Huff in her underwear. Can you even imagine?"

"*Eww!*" everyone shrieks at the same time, and then all five of us crack up. Laughing is even better than the deep breathing, and my chest loosens some more. It practically feels normal now.

"Sorry we didn't tell you this earlier," Tess says. "But you kept saying you were fine."

"It's okay."

Mariah hands me a water bottle—where was she hiding *that*?—and I drink some. "How come you're so calm?" I ask her. "You've never done this before either."

She shrugs. "I have to speak in front of people all the time for student council and stuff. I guess I'm used to it. Plus I like it when everyone pays attention to me."

"News flash," Tess says, and Faith and Claudia laugh.

"I freak out about other stuff, though," Mariah says. "I'm terrified of heights. I almost didn't sign up to run the decorating committee because I thought I might have to get on a ladder."

I expect Tess to make fun of Mariah some more, but instead she turns back to me. "Feeling any better?"

"Yeah, thanks," I say, and I mean it. It's weird how comforting these girls are, even though I don't know them that well. Usually, Sydney's the only one who can calm me down. But maybe that's because I've never given anyone else a chance to try. Syd's my best friend, but she doesn't really understand what I'm going through tonight. Even if she were here, she might not know the right things to say, like Tess and Faith and Claudia do.

I've always thought that being someone's best friend meant being *everything* to them—someone to laugh with and cry with and entrust with every single one of your secrets. I've always tried to be that for Syd. But she needed new people anyway, and maybe I deserve to have other people too.

"Come sit up here," Faith says. "I'll redo your makeup."

I get up, and my legs don't shake at all as I walk over and perch next to Faith on the edge of the stage. She wets one of Mariah's tissues and wipes my cheeks, and it comes away black with melted mascara. Then she pulls out a makeup bag.

"Put the silver eyeliner on her," Claudia says. "It'll look awesome with her skin."

Faith nods. "Oooh, yeah, good call. Close your eyes, Gen."

The slow, gentle strokes of the pencil are soothing, and I sit very still as Faith lines my eyes. I stay quiet as the rest of the girls talk and laugh around me, but I don't feel separate now, the way I did when we were in the chorus room. I'm as much a part of the group as they are.

"There," Faith says when she's finished with my makeup. "What do you think?" She pulls out her phone and opens the front-facing camera so I can see myself. My eyes look huge and sparkly and metallic, and my lips are a shiny dark red, the color of the wine Papa drinks on special occasions. Faith did an amazing job, but it's a pretty out-there look for me.

"You don't think it's too much?" I turn around so the rest of the girls can see.

"It's perfect," Tess says. "Stage makeup is supposed to be dramatic. Now you look like the rock star you are."

I look down at the floor. "I'm not a rock star."

"Um, you definitely are," says Faith. "You're the lead singer in a rock band. That's the literal definition of 'rock star.'"

"Only for tonight." I glance back up at Tess. "Speaking of that, is Carmen going to be mad about, um . . . what happened earlier? Do you think she'll kick me out of the band?"

Tess looks confused. "What? Of course not. Why would she do that?"

"I mean, I don't think she likes me that much to begin with, and she seemed so mad that I was singing tonight, and when I texted her earlier, she didn't even write back, so I thought—"

"She's just upset that she's at her cousin's wedding," Tess says. "It has nothing to do with you. She thinks you're great. The second you walked out of your audition, she was like,

'Yup, that's the one—she's amazing.' Six more people sang after you, but Carmen had already made up her mind."

Warmth radiates out from my middle, like I'm suddenly full of hot cocoa and marshmallows. "Really? I . . . I didn't know that."

Ms. Huff pokes her head backstage, and everyone remembers the underwear comment and starts laughing again. "There's going to be another opening in the broadcast in a couple of minutes," she says. "I'm really sorry for the disruption. Are you ready?"

Everyone nods, and Tess looks at me. "You good to go?"

"Yes," I say. And even though I'm still scared, this time I'm telling the truth.

"Great. You can come out onstage now. Take your cues from the cameraman and Mr. Stanwick like last time, okay? Break a leg, ladies!"

There's no time for the preshow ritual now, but Tess holds out her arms, and we all smoosh together. "Talented and unafraid!" she yells. "Who are we?"

"WE'RE HEART GRENADE!" I shout along with the other girls.

Everyone starts screaming the second we walk out onstage

again, and at first, it's just like before. My heart pounds as I plant my feet on that pink X on the floor, and my chest starts to seize up as I stare into the bright lights. But I take deep breaths like Tess showed me, and I soften my knees like Faith said. And then I sneak a tiny peek over my shoulder at my bandmates, and when they all smile back at me, it's suddenly nothing like before. I'm the one at the front of the stage, pinned in the white-hot spotlight, but I'm not up here alone. I'm part of something much bigger than myself.

I watch the cameraman as he counts down on his fingers and points at Mr. Stanwick. "And now," our vice principal says again, "I give you Heart Grenade, winner of the Lynnfield Mall Battle of the Bands, making their television debut!"

"One! Two! One, two, three, four!" Tess shouts.

She starts pounding out the opening of "Hear Us Roar," but they're not plain old drumbeats anymore—in her rhythm, I hear *You can DO it you can DO it you can DO it you can DO it!*

Faith joins in with a few low bass notes, and I hear *Goooooo, Gennnnnn! Goooooo, Gennnnnn!*

Their music makes me brave, and when I raise my head and look out into the crowd, I spot Sydney standing about halfway back on the left side, gripping Kevin's hand as she cheers us on.

She's not front and center like she promised, but it doesn't sting quite as much as I expect. This performance isn't about her and me; there will be time for us to work things out later, when we're alone. The next four minutes are about me and my new friends, the ones who are willing to stand behind me and back me up.

My cue comes, and when I open my mouth, my voice flies out like it can't wait to escape, full and sweet and strong. It glides over my cheering classmates, turns loops over the teachers and the cameraman, and soars out through the airwaves to Dad and Papa and my choir director and the rest of the town. I can almost feel the band smiling behind me.

Tess was right. Tonight, I *am* a rock star.

CARMEN { 10:27 P.M. }

THERE ARE CERTAIN THINGS IN LIFE I'll never admit. Like how I sucked my thumb until I was eight. Or how when I'm bored, I like to do math problems for fun. Or the time I accidentally farted in fifth grade and everyone blamed Marty Thompson and called him Farty Marty for months.

And I'll never, ever admit that Genevieve sounds kind of sort of maybe a teeny bit good singing with Heart Grenade.

I mean, her vocal style is totally different from mine, and there was that point before the lights went off when I could tell she'd forgotten the words, but as a replacement, she isn't that bad.

{ 284 }

"I love this song!" Alex says. He bounces up and down with Lucas to the beat of "Hear Us Roar."

"Heart Grenade is rocking it tonight," Lucas tells me.

I eye him suspiciously. Does he mean they're good because I'm not performing with them?

"That girl is pretty awesome," Lucas says, and yep, there it is. They think Genevieve is a better singer than me.

I wait for the insult to come.

But it doesn't happen.

Instead, Lucas continues to talk. "I mean, she's good, but she's got nothing on you. The band sounds even better when you're singing lead vocals."

"He's right!" Alex chimes in before they go back to dancing to the music.

"The band sounds great," Jackson agrees. "Maybe I can get my parents to drive me to see you perform with them sometime."

Wait, what?! Jackson wants to see me again after the wedding?! My insides do a crazy happy dance, but outside, I try to play it cool.

"That would be nice," I tell him in a small voice that makes me sound totally uncool.

But he grins back, and a giggle bubbles out of my mouth that I don't even try to hide.

"Heart Grenade is my new favorite band," Lucas exclaims as he pumps his fist in the air.

And here's one more thing that I'll never, ever admit: Maybe my family isn't so bad after all.

RYAN { 10:28 P.M. }

AMANDA HAS A DIMPLE ON EITHER SIDE of her mouth. You can't really see them until she smiles. But she smiles a lot, especially when I pay attention to her.

"Mr. Thomas," Amanda says as we wait for the concert to start. "How boring is he?"

"I guess it would be hard for anyone to make exponential equations fun and interesting," I joke.

Amanda laughs. She's laughed at every other jokey comment I've made so far. I like that about her. Plus, I feel relaxed talking to her, now that I'm over my initial nervousness.

All that was forgotten as soon as Mariah stepped onstage.

I can't take my eyes off my best friend as she sings into the microphone and moves to the music. I'm sure everyone else in the room notices the way she lights up that stage.

"Mariah is doing a great job," Amanda says as we stand there watching Heart Grenade perform. I wonder if she says that because she realizes my eyes have been on Mariah the whole time.

"She is," I say, turning to smile at Amanda, who really *is* cute. And she hasn't put me in the friend zone. At least I don't *think* she has.

I've spent so long crushing on Mariah, I haven't really noticed girls like Amanda. Maybe I should start. But before I can do that, I need to settle things with Mariah.

I haven't felt right since speaking to her before the performance. I started dancing with Amanda to make Mariah jealous, but after a few minutes, we were laughing and having a good time, and I kind of forgot about Mariah until I saw her onstage.

As I stand here, I realize that this whole jerk act isn't me. Mariah and I need to get things back to where we were at the beginning of the night. If that means she'll never think of me as more than a friend, fine. It's better than having her hate me for being mean.

"Thank you, everyone!" Genevieve says into the microphone, and I realize that Heart Grenade is finished. That means Mariah will be coming off that stage. She should see a friendly face when she does.

"Excuse me," I say to Amanda. "I'll be right back. Just have to congratulate my best friend."

I walk toward the stage. The band members wave at the audience as they head for the stairs. Tess and Mariah are at the back of the group. If I go straight there, I can meet Mariah when she comes down.

But I can't greet her empty-handed. I need flowers or a glass of punch or something to give her as a peace offering. I see something even better than punch on the refreshments table: cupcakes . . . and the icing is purple, Mariah's favorite color.

I grab one, then try to squeeze through the crowd that has gathered near the edge of the stage. Heart Grenade is famous!

"Hey, Ryan," Faith says as she breezes past me. She's quickly surrounded by a bunch of people kissing up to her. The good news is, by the time Mariah and Tess make it to the bottom of the stairs, the group has moved away, giving me a fair shot at Mariah.

Only she doesn't make eye contact with me. She acts like I'm not even standing there.

"Mariah!" I call out.

She says something to Tess, then turns to me with a stony expression on her face.

"I just wanted to say I'm sorry." I hold out the cupcake to her.

"Uh-huh." Her arms are crossed firmly across her chest.

"I was acting like a jerk earlier," I say.

"Yep."

Okay, so maybe I didn't think this one through. I can't explain why I was being a jerk without coming right out and saying that I like her.

"Look," she says, dropping her arms and looking around. "I know, all right?"

"Know?" I ask, suddenly feeling sick to my stomach.

"I *know* know," she says, avoiding my eyes. She shifts from one foot to the other. "It's just . . . you're like a brother to me. I don't even want to like guys *that way* right now, and when I do like one, it's weird. But our friendship *isn't* weird. It's real. That's better than being my boyfriend, because you're my *always* friend."

I want to drop the cupcake at her feet and run as far and as fast as my feet will carry me. But I don't. Instead, I take a deep breath and I try to hear what she's saying. Boyfriends don't always last. Best friends do.

But that's only if I can start being a real friend.

What can I do? If she doesn't feel *that way* about me, she doesn't. I'd rather have her in my life as a friend than nothing at all.

"Okay," I finally say. "Friends?"

I don't completely mean it now, but in a while I might. It's worth a try anyway.

I hold the cupcake toward her. She looks down, a big smile breaks across her face, and she takes it.

"*Best* friends," she says.

TESS { 10:31 P.M. }

SO THIS IS WHAT BEING A REAL ROCK STAR IS like. The second we finished playing—before we could even jump off the stage—we were swarmed. And despite the rough start, people *loved* us. So much so that there are still a bunch of kids hanging around, never mind that we finished three minutes ago.

When Mariah said that someone had sabotaged the show, I was, well . . . *not* happy. More like the polar opposite of happy. Even though the lights going out was probably the best thing that could've happened for Gen at that moment, and everything turned out okay (or really, better than okay), if I find out who's responsible, heads will roll.

For now, I give a funny look to a girl in marching band who asks if Heart Grenade needs a clarinet player. And I check my phone. There's a text from Carmen. I wish she were here. Without her, the night is just a tiny bit less than perfect.

Thx!! Not the same without you. ☹

I hit send on the text and make my way around the edge of the stage to Mariah and Ryan.

"Hey!" Mariah says, purple frosting dotting her upper lip.

"Hi . . ." I raise my eyebrows at Ryan, a.k.a. her best friend who was acting like a jerk to her earlier. She told me all about it while we waited backstage. I can't believe I thought he might like her. And I really can't believe I care about Mariah's feelings.

"Everything's okay," Mariah says with a little smile.

I give Ryan a look, just in case he gets any ideas about acting that way again. "If you say so."

"Really, it is." Mariah stares at her purple cupcake. "I . . . I wanted to say thank you."

"To him?" I ask. Ryan shrinks a little bit.

"No, weirdo, you." She rolls her eyes, and for a moment, she looks like the old Mariah. The one who would've marched

{ 293 }

up to me after the show and told me she could've played the drums ten times better than I had.

"Um . . . you're welcome?" I tap out a cymbal pattern on my thigh. This is all just a little . . . strange.

Mariah grins. "You're the one who let me be part of the group tonight. And I *loved* it." She pauses. "Your face! You look like no one's ever thanked you before."

Actually, no one does. Not very often, anyway. Then again, "nice girl" is hardly my middle name. Tess "Nice Girl" Emrich. Okay, no. That sounds ridiculous. But . . . I am leaving this dance with two new friends: Genevieve . . . and Mariah, the one girl I never thought would be a friend.

Maybe I should try this being-nice thing a little more often.

"You're welcome," I say to Mariah again. At least it doesn't sound like a question this time. "You know, sometimes Heart Grenade could use two backup singers. If you're interested, anyway."

She smiles. "Yeah. I might be." She breaks off a piece of that electric purple cupcake and holds it out to me.

"Thank you," I say as I take it.

She blinks at me. "You're . . . welcome." Mariah almost trips over the words.

We both start cracking up.

"I don't get it," Ryan says. That makes us laugh harder.

When I finally catch my breath, I hand him my phone and make him take a picture of me and Mariah, arms around each other's shoulders, a bite of cupcake in each of our free hands. Carmen is going to *die* when she sees this. I hit send on the text. Right away, my phone dings.

DID YOU LOSE A BET?!? 😵

I laugh as I type back to her.

Nah. Just that Leif's parents sold the bank and Ashlyn donated her designer clothes to charity and Mariah isn't all that bad.

Are you being held hostage? Type 1 for yes and 2 for no.

M might join the band.

You're being blackmailed. Right?

☺ ☺ ☺

This is so weird.

I drop my phone back into my boot at the same time Faith plows into me from behind. "Can you even *believe* this night!" she shouts.

Mariah and I turn around and find the rest of the band—all smiles and energy and excitement.

"Best. Show. Ever!" Claudia says.

"A kid from the chess club asked me for my autograph," Genevieve says, sounding kind of dazed.

"You totally said no, right?" I tease her.

Worry flits across her face. "No . . . wait, am I supposed to?"

"No, goofball." I bump her shoulder with mine. "Of course not. I'm just messing with you."

"Oh." Then she grins. "Oh!" she says with a laugh.

"Seriously, you guys. This was the *best* night ever!" I say to everyone. "Even with the power issue. Although if anyone finds out who did that . . ."

The cameraman from the station is walking toward us, two kids practically hanging off either side of him.

"It's another one of your fans, Gen." Faith elbows Genevieve, who turns so red I can actually see it on her brown skin.

"Hi, girls," he says, a little girl hanging from each arm. "I'm Garrett Terzetti. I run the cameras for the station. Nice job up there."

"Thanks," Mariah says. And her grin could light up the gym scoreboard.

"I'm really sorry about what happened with the lights. It—"

"Wait, it was *your* fault? Do you know how hard we

worked?" I ball my hands into fists at my sides. How dare this guy almost ruin our big chance!

He pulls a hand free of one of the girls and holds it up. "I didn't say that. What I was going to say is that it wasn't the station's fault. But we feel awful about it, and my niece is insisting we make it up to you." He points behind him.

I have no idea who he's talking about, even after I lean to the side to see where he's pointing. Everyone else in the band does the same. There's a girl in a green dress, standing behind the video equipment, giving us a halfhearted wave. I've never seen her before.

She leans over and snags the shirtsleeve of a boy with a camera—a fancy, expensive-looking camera. One that looks pricey enough to keep me in non-Mom-approved clip-in hair streaks for all time. But this kid with the camera . . . he looks familiar. I realize it's the same guy who jumped out of the stall in the haunted bathroom and snapped that picture of me and Mariah earlier. I vaguely recognize him as an eighth grader on the yearbook committee. He's walking over to us now, but the girl stays behind. There's something about her. I narrow my eyes, trying to figure it out, but I can't.

I turn back to Mr. Terzetti. "You were saying something about making it up to us?"

"Yes, I've checked with the station manager, and we'd love to have you on *Wake Up, Lynnfield* next week if you're interested."

Wake Up, Lynnfield. The morning show. Us. Heart Grenade. What?! I look at Mariah, who looks at Faith, who looks at Claudia, who looks at Genevieve.

"Yes!" we all shout at practically the same time.

"Also, the yearbook photographer has offered to take your picture," says Mr. Terzetti.

"We want our pictures taken too!" one of the little kids says.

"He already took our picture," I say, more to the yearbook kid than to Mr. Terzetti.

"And if we see that particular picture in the yearbook, Tess and I will personally seek you out and let you know *exactly* how we feel about it," Mariah adds.

I have to work really, really hard not to smile. Just think— all these years trying to one-up Mariah when I could have had her on my side.

Then I guess the guy finally finds his voice, because he says, "This is different. Half the town saw your band on TV tonight. I bet you'll be getting calls to play everywhere now. And what famous band doesn't have a professional portrait? You'll need one to give out to . . . important band-type people." He messes with the strap on his camera. "And I promise to delete the other picture."

I look at the girls. One by one, they shrug or smile or nod. It's not an all-expenses-paid trip to Los Angeles or anything, but I have to admit, a good picture of us would be nice. Except . . .

"Carmen isn't here," I tell them. "She's our usual lead singer."

The boy waves his hand. "No problem. I'll Photoshop her in."

"I guess we're all set, then." Mr. Terzetti grabs a kid in each hand and strides back through the crowd.

The girl in the green dress watches us for a moment longer. Then I could swear she gives me half a smile before she disappears after her uncle.

So. Weird.

But I don't have time to wonder who she is or why she wanted to make up the power outage to us, because everyone else is already back onstage. Mariah stays below to direct the shot. Which is basically the perfect spot for her since she's always been good at bossing people around. She tells Faith to stand more to the left and Gen to look more fierce. Then she goes back and forth over whether I should sit or stand behind the drums. I finally tell her to stuff it, and I stand next to the drums, one foot propped on an amp. And then I tell her to get her butt onto the stage to be in the picture too.

Before I know it, the yearbook guy's taken a bunch of shots. While everyone's checking out the shots on his camera, Mariah grabs my arm and pulls me aside.

"Option C," she says with an evil grin.

"Option C," I repeat.

And with that, she heads off in one direction while I make my way through the crowd on the dance floor. In no time flat, I find who I'm looking for.

Leif.

ELLIE { **10:46 P.M.** }

SOO-JIN'S CAR PULLS UP IN FRONT OF the school. We're the only ones out front; everyone else is still at the dance. Ashlyn heads right for the front passenger-side door, like always. She has her hand on the handle when she turns to look at me.

"Do you want to sit in the front?"

"What?" I'm about to open my own door to get into the seat behind hers.

"I mean, I always have the front. Just figured you might want a turn."

"Oh," I say. "Oh, wow. That's really nice of you to think of me like—"

"Do you want the front or not?" Ashlyn rubs her hands together. "It's getting cold out here."

"Thank you for asking," I say, "but I'm fine in the back."

"Whatevs." Ashlyn looks over my shoulder, eyes wide at whatever is behind me, then ducks into the car.

"Ashlyn?" Soo-jin frowns. "What are you doing here? You're supposed to be babysitting."

"Oh, that." Ashlyn waves her hands in front of her face, her words coming fast. "Funny story. I'll tell you later. We should get going. We don't want to block traffic."

I jump when someone knocks on Soo-jin's window. She rolls it down, and standing there is Mr. Terzetti. His face is red, and the vein in his forehead is throbbing.

"Soo-jin. We need to talk." He glares at Ashlyn. "Alone."

Ashlyn slides down in her seat and groans.

Soo-jin says something to Mr. Terzetti, rolls her window up, and pulls into a parking spot.

"Is there something you'd like to tell me before I speak to Mr. Terzetti, Ashlyn?" Soo-jin's lips are pursed so tightly that I'm not sure how words are coming out of them.

"Yes." Ashlyn sits up in her seat. "It wasn't my fault."

"We'll see about that." Soo-jin slams the car door and meets Mr. Terzetti on the sidewalk.

"I don't see what the problem is," Ashlyn says without taking her eyes off of her mom and Mr. Terzetti. "The twins had a total blast. And nobody got hurt. Much."

"As long as everybody's safe, that's all that matters," I say, even though I was completely shocked and slightly horrified to see the twins at the dance. Especially since I know how protective the Terzettis are. Ashlyn's going to be in big trouble.

Soo-jin speed-walks back to the car, opens the door, and parks herself in the driver's seat. Her arms are crossed, and she's staring straight ahead. No one speaks for a full minute.

"I don't know what to say." Soo-jin shakes her head as she pulls out of the parking lot. "You took the twins to the dance? Do you know how irresponsible that was and how dangerous it could have been?"

"But it wasn't!" Ashlyn gives Soo-jin a smile. "And the twins had an awesome night. One they'll never forget."

"You can't even admit your mistake! Just the fact that you went to the dance while grounded is bad enough, but you took *children* with you! Children that you were responsible for!" Soo-jin is yelling now. "What do I have to do to make an impact on you?"

Ashlyn tries to interrupt, but Soo-jin puts her hand up and continues, "We will have a serious talk about this later. But I'll tell you one thing. Expect to be grounded for quite a while, young lady."

"Don't worry, Ashlyn," I pipe up from the backseat. "I barely ever leave the house anyway, so we can binge-watch season three of *Secret Lives of Celebrity Sisters* together."

Soo-jin looks in the rearview mirror and notices me for the first time since I got in the car. "Ellie, you do not have to do that. Ashlyn made a huge mistake, and . . ." Her eyes flash downward. "Honey, what are you wearing? What happened to your beautiful dress?"

"There was a little accident," I say. This makes Ashlyn giggle, and then I giggle, and pretty soon we're both cracking up and I'm bent over my seat laughing so hard my stomach starts to hurt.

"I'm okay," I say before Soo-jin can ask. I hold up the plastic bag that has my dress in it. "And so is my dress. At least it will be."

"What in the world happened tonight?" Soo-jin keeps

looking back and forth between Ashlyn and me, her brows furrowed.

"How funny was it when I thought that Jade girl was beating you up?" Ashlyn asks.

This makes me laugh so hard I snort. Soo-jin doesn't find it so humorous.

"What?" Soo-jin's eyes flash in the rearview mirror. "Someone tried to beat you up?"

"No, Mom," Ashlyn says in between guffaws. "I *thought* she was getting beat up. But really, she stopped someone from sabotaging the band and just slipped on the soap-covered floor during the blackout!"

"What on earth—" Soo-jin begins, but Ashlyn cuts her off.

"It was epic, Mom." Ashlyn turns around in the front seat to look at me. "And did you see the look on Kevin's face when we paraded by him? I could tell that he loves your new look, Ells."

"Do you really think he noticed?"

"Totally," Ashlyn says. "And this is only the beginning. We're going to have him drooling over you by the end of the month, and when he asks you out for real, you can humiliate him all over social media."

"I don't even have a phone," I remind her.

"Fine. Then *I'll* humiliate him all over social media." Ashlyn claps. She sounds downright giddy.

"I have no idea what's going on here." Soo-jin sighs. "But it's nice to see you girls laughing together."

Ashlyn and I give each other a quick glance, and then we giggle some more.

"Don't think this will get you off the hook, young lady," Soo-jin says. "You're still grounded. For a long, long time."

When we pull into the garage, Soo-jin gets out of the car, and Ashlyn turns around to me. "Ugh. I have a feeling we'll have plenty of time to watch all the seasons of *Celebrity Sisters* when Mr. Terzetti finds out about the Munchinator."

"Oh no, Ashlyn." I put my palms over my eyes. "Don't tell me something happened to the Munchinator. Mr. Terzetti adores that lawn mower more than his own car!"

Ashlyn scrunches up her nose. "I'm sure someone can fix it. Maybe."

And even though I know she's going to be in more trouble, I burst out laughing, which makes Ashlyn laugh too.

"Don't worry." Ashlyn and I head into the house. "I'll fill you in on the entire story. It's a good one."

We climb up the steps, and as we're about to go into

our respective bedrooms, we pause. I pull the headband that Soo-jin gave me out of my hair and hand it to Ashlyn.

"I believe this is yours."

Ashlyn looks at it for a second, but then shakes her head. "I'm not sure my mom—"

"But it belonged to your . . . harmoni?"

Ashlyn laughs. "*Halmoni.* Not bad, though; you were close. I can teach you some Korean if you want."

"Okay, but then how will you complain about me behind my back?"

"Right. Good point." But she winks so I know she's joking.

She carefully takes the headband from me and holds it between her fingers. "Thanks. I'm glad you got to wear it tonight."

"Good night, Ashlyn."

"Good night, Ells."

I close my bedroom door and twirl around in my room. There's no dress. No fancy shoes. No daydreams of Kevin. There's just me.

But there's also Ashlyn, right down the hall.

Just as I'm about to open my journal and write all about tonight's events, there's a knock on my door.

"Come in," I say, placing my journal on my nightstand.

Soo-jin opens the door slowly. "Do you have a minute?"

"Sure." I sit down on my bed.

"I hope you don't think I'm intruding, but I'm a bit concerned about the accident you and Ashlyn were discussing." She sits next to me on the bed. "And, truth be told, I wanted to know how your night was."

"My night was . . ." I search my mind for just the right word. "Unexpected."

"Oh?" Soo-jin raises her eyebrows.

"My date with Kevin was a disaster." Even as I say these words, I don't feel nearly as much of the humiliation, or shame, or any of those icky feelings I felt when Kevin told me that asking me to the dance was nothing more than a joke.

"I'm so sorry." Soo-jin looks like she's about to cry. "I know how much this meant to you."

"It did mean a lot to me," I say. "But maybe for the wrong reasons."

"How so?" Soo-jin asks.

"I think I was looking for a friend. I've never really had a true friend." I chuckle. "At least not one that I didn't write myself."

I glance up at Soo-jin. She's nodding.

"But that may have changed tonight."

"With Ashlyn?" Soo-jin's entire face shines, like there's a lightbulb behind her smile.

"For one." I grin. "We had a good time together."

"I'm glad to hear it." Soo-jin pats my knee. "But she and I just spoke, and I made it very clear that she's still grounded."

"Don't be too hard on her," I say. "At least I won't have to compete with her for babysitting jobs."

"That's for sure." Soo-jin shakes her head, but she's laughing softly.

"Thanks for all your help tonight," I say. "It meant a lot to me, you know, to have someone to talk to."

Soo-jin takes my hand. "I'm honored to have the opportunity."

We sit in silence for a few seconds, until Soo-jin stands up. "It's late, and I'm guessing you're tired. What do you say you give me that dress and I'll hang it in the bathroom to dry? Then tomorrow, we'll take it to the cleaners."

I pull the dress out of the plastic bag and hand it to Soo-jin. Her nose scrunches up as she takes it.

"That's some seriously stinky soap," she says.

I shrug. "At least it isn't dirty."

"Good night, Ellie." Soo-jin gives me a kiss on the cheek. "See you in the morning."

I get into my pajamas and fold Ashlyn's clothes neatly on the chair in my room. When I woke up this morning, I never would have guessed that I would end my day wearing an Ashlyn outfit, which, surprisingly enough, I thought looked pretty good on me.

A smile creeps across my face as I crawl into bed and pull the covers up to my chin. A warmth starts in my chest and soon fills my entire body. I remember this feeling from when I was a little kid and I would snuggle with my parents in their big bed as they read me bedtime stories. It's a feeling of belonging. It's a feeling of being loved.

I open my journal and begin to write:

Although the dance didn't go at all as I expected, it was even better than I dreamed it would be. I stood up for myself, and for Heart Grenade. I made a friend. And most important, I'm part of a family again.

I don't know what will happen on Monday. Kevin might still be mean. The popular girls might still ignore me. But I know one thing that will be different.

Me.

TESS { 11:10 P.M. }

I LEAN OH-SO-CASUALLY AGAINST THE open gym doors while I go to town shaking a can of Diet Coke. Ryan found a whole case of it under the refreshment table (who knew the chaperones had their own stash of drinks?). He also found a few other useful things in the boxes the decorating committee stored in the janitor's closet.

I shake the can again, just for good measure, and then I hide it behind my back. I study the rope snaking its way up and over the open door. Mariah and I owe Ryan big-time for that. He was thisclose to getting caught, but Mariah managed to head off the chaperone with a fake overflowing toilet emergency in the haunted bathroom.

The dance officially ended at eleven, but kids are slowly making their way out the doors. I texted Mom and told her to pick me up a little later so I could help the decorating committee take everything down. Which isn't *exactly* the truth, but Operation Make Leif Regret His Life Choices is so worth a teeny, tiny lie.

Directing a group of kids from the soccer team through one of the other open doors, I wave at the girls in the band. They're all clumped off to the side, watching to see what Mariah and I cooked up. Ryan hovers next to them, hands in his pockets and a smile on his face. Faith holds up her phone, Carmen waiting on FaceTime. It took some work—she had to borrow a phone with a decent signal from one of the other bridesmaids—but it's going to be worth it. No way was Carmen missing out on *this*.

They don't have to wait long, because I spot Leif moving this way. I paste on my sweetest smile, which actually hurts a little. Mariah's got him by the hand and is chattering on and on about who only knows what. Leif's nodding and looking around, like he's trying to find a way to escape her.

He'll wish he'd escaped her—and me—by the time this is done.

When they get close enough, I move into the doorway.

"Leif!" I wave furiously at him.

His eyes widen, and he tries to stop, but Mariah tugs him along, still talking up a storm.

"Ex-CUSE me, Tess," Mariah says when they get to the door. "Leif and I need to go wait for our parents."

"But I brought him a drink." I brandish the Diet Coke like it's Christmas and Halloween and his birthday, all wrapped up in one. "Sorry I couldn't find anything better, but you've got to be thirsty after all that dancing and . . . hiding."

"I—" Leif says, but Mariah pulls him right under the door frame. Exactly where we want him.

I thrust the drink under his nose. "I totally stole this from the chaperones." I pout. "You can't not drink it now."

And before he can say anything else, I take a step back, tilt the can toward him, and pop the lid open. Mariah scoots away just in time. The sticky, brown liquid shoots everywhere—including all over Leif.

Mission accomplished.

It's all over my hands, too, but I don't really care. It feels like sweet, sweet (artificially sweet, but still) revenge.

"Oops," I say in a voice that's not really sorry at all. I have to bite my lip to keep from laughing.

Diet Coke drips off the ends of Leif's blond hair into his eyes. He blinks and then runs his hands over his face. "Wh . . . ? Agggh! Tess!"

"I'm sorry. I guess it fell on the floor. Or something." Just as the last words leave my mouth, Mariah reaches for the rope hanging from the top of the doorway. I step away. She slides back even farther . . . and pulls.

The bucket Ryan rigged for us at the top of the door jerks sideways, and shiny, shimmery glitter rains down onto Leif's head. And his shoulders. And his polo shirt. And, well, everywhere. He's basically a frozen, sputtering, multicolored glitter statue.

A giggle travels up into my throat. I force it down. Tess Emrich does not giggle. She does, however, laugh like a hyena with Mariah.

And before Leif can make for the bathroom, Mariah and I sidle up to him. I whip my phone out in front of the three of us and snap a shot as Mariah and I each give Leif a peck on his glittery cheeks. I'm just barely aware of the crowd that's starting to form around us. *This* is going to go viral on Instagram. My fingers fly over the screen.

Best. Night. Ever.

"Next time," I say to Leif once the picture is posted, "don't say yes to two girls."

"Especially if those two girls are us," Mariah adds.

Leif finally unfreezes. He glares at us. "Don't you dare post that anywhere!"

"Sorry not sorry. Too late." I show him my phone.

"I. Can't. Believe. This!" He stomps off toward the bathroom, leaving a glitter trail in his wake. I take one look at Mariah, and we're both cackling again, so hard I can barely breathe. Ryan and the girls in Heart Grenade manage to grab us by the elbows and tug us off to the side before the chaperones find us.

Faith holds up her phone. There's Carmen, laughing so hard that she's wiping away tears. Next to her is Jackson, laughing just as much even though he doesn't even know us or Leif. And shoved in behind them is someone I'm guessing is the bridesmaid who owns the phone. Even she's laughing.

"That?" Carmen says. "Was *perfect*."

I sling an arm around Mariah and grin. "It was pretty

great. But it would've been more perfect with you here."

Her eyes flick to Jackson. Then she gives the camera a little grin. "That's okay. I think I'm exactly where I'm supposed to be tonight."

I miss her, but maybe she's right.

Maybe we're all exactly where we're supposed to be tonight.

ACKNOWLEDGMENTS

Seven sets of arms around Amy Cloud, our fearless editor, for her cheerful response when we first proposed a multiauthored novel . . . and for everything that has come since. You are a marvel! Best. Experience. Ever.

More hugs to the entire Aladdin team, including Mara Anastas, Janet Rosenberg, Chelsea Morgan, Karin Paprocki, Mike Rosamilia, illustrator James Lopez, Sara Berko, and the unsung heroes of sales and marketing, who trumpet our books' arrivals into the world. We are crazy grateful for all of your support!

Holly Root, thank you for your agenting prowess on

this one—it does not go unnoticed or unappreciated!

A giant round of applause to our middle school focus group, made up of the fabulous Olivia Seifrick, Colin Hunter, Maddie Tuck, Julianna Singer, Michelle Rayner, Belle Scarano, Caroline Malone, Ingrid Thullen, Anna Tracey, Isadora DaSilva, Morgan Macdougal, and Mary O'Dee's grandchildren: Maeve and Fiona Walsh, Grace, Jack and Molly Whalen, and Colin McLeod. Yay to your awesome feedback and brainstorming!

And now for some individual thanks:

RACHELE ALPINE

A million thanks to my amazing agent, Natalie Lakosil—you rock as much as Heart Grenade at a middle school dance! Thank you to Lili Aguilera, Sonia Rodriguez, and Kelly Holderman for your awesome knowledge and help with creating the character of Carmen and her world. Thank you to the band Boyz II Men, whose song "End of the Road" played during my first-ever slow dance in eighth grade—my hands might have been sweaty and I was a nervous wreck, but I'll never forget that moment! Love to my coauthors . . . Who knew telling seven sides to this story would be so fun?! And as always, endless love and thanks to my family, who know how to bust a move on the dance floor at any family wedding!

ACKNOWLEDGMENTS

RONNI ARNO

As always, big thanks to my incredible agent and all-around wonderful person, Sarah Davies. Thanks also to my brilliant coauthors Rachele Alpine, Alison Cherry, Stephanie Faris, Jen Malone, Gail Nall, and Dee Romito. This book would not be possible without every single one of you. I also need to give a shout-out to Andy Chek, my middle school dance partner and forever friend. And, of course, love and gratitude to my parents; my husband, Josh; and my amazing kids, Hallie and Morgan.

ALISON CHERRY

Thanks to Baker Demonstration School, where I spent three surprisingly happy (if angsty) years of middle school—I have a crystal clear memory of our seventh-grade dance, during which the teachers bribed us to dance by passing out quarters. Thank you to all my glorious writer friends, who keep me sane as I put my characters through the wringer. And the biggest thanks of all to my family, who knew me as a seventh grader and somehow still love me.

STEPHANIE FARIS

A big thanks to my agent, Natalie Lakosil, for always steering me in the right direction, especially when I'm distracted by bright,

ACKNOWLEDGMENTS

shiny ideas. Also a big thanks to my husband, who helped give me insight into how a young guy thinks, since I had absolutely no idea when I started writing.

JEN MALONE

Much love and thanks to Tae Keller for the sensitivity read on Ashlyn's character—any mistakes are my own. A second thanks to my agent, Holly Root—don't worry, I remember my blood oath. Special thanks to the Girl Scouts of Eastern MA for always supporting my books. Apologies to any boy whose feet I stepped on as we slow-danced—I'd say I've gotten better . . . but nope. John, thanks for being the only guy I dance with these days, even if it's usually just around the kitchen island. Thanks to Jack, Ben, and Caroline for endless inspiration and letting me relive school drama through your eyes. And to my megatalented coauthors: I'd write anything with you girls, anytime.

GAIL NALL

Huge thanks to my favorite (and only!) agent, Julia A. Weber, who has Tess's guts, Ellie's smarts, Ashlyn's style, Jade's tenacity, Ryan's heart, Genevieve's fearlessness, and Carmen's patience. Shout-out to my coauthors—you all made this experience seven times more fun than writing by myself! Another big thank-you goes out to Mike Grosso, who made sure Tess sounds like a real drummer (any mistakes are all on me!). Thanks to my own grade school, St. Bartholomew, for giving me years and years' worth of middle school drama to write about. To my family and friends—thank you for being there for me. As always, Eva, this is for you.

DEE ROMITO

Big thanks to my wonderful agent, Uwe Stender, who is an absolute rock star and is always cheering me on. To Sweet Home Middle, for all those blue-and-gold dances, and for your continued (and much appreciated) support. To my six amazing coauthors—who knew a dance planning committee could be so fun? And an enormous, heartfelt thank-you to my incredible friends, my family, my mom and dad, my husband, and my kids, Nathan and Kiley—I am always and forever grateful that every day you make life something to dance to.

AN INTERVIEW WITH THE AUTHORS

Sometime shortly after we turned in the final version of *Best. Night. Ever.* to our editor, we met online for a video chat to talk about the process. To set the scene: Ronni shows up onscreen with her new puppy barking loudly in the background. Gail has cut shorter bangs since the last time we all video-chatted, and we pause to ooh and aah over them. Rachele proceeds to paint her nails a sparkly red as we wait for the rest of our crew to log in, claiming now that she has a toddler it's the only chance she has to sit still long enough for them to dry without smudges. We all tease her, and then take a poll to see who is dressed for a video chat on the top, but secretly wearing pajamas on the bottom. Seven out of seven of us raise a hand. (Jen stands to show everyone that hers have little hedgehogs on them.)

And then we're off, with Jen tossing out the questions.

So, Best. Night. Ever. *is a novel told from seven perspectives, with each of us writing one character's chapters. It's a pretty unique project in that respect—how did you feel when I first approached you about the idea?*

RONNI: Best. Idea. Ever. I loved the idea, and couldn't wait to get started.

STEPHANIE: I was so excited to work with other middle grade authors. I'd read all of your books and admired you as writers, so from the start, it felt like I was part of something big!

RACHELE: Seven authors writing one book together sounded crazy to me, but I love a good challenge, so I was definitely thinking, "Bring it! Let's do this!"

AN INTERVIEW WITH THE AUTHORS

ALISON: I definitely thought, "I HAVE to join this project—I can't let all these ladies have fun WITHOUT me!" (Writer FOMO??)

Steph, you mentioned that we all have our own books out in the world and, not coincidentally, we all write for the same imprint at the same publisher. Our books share a really similar vibe to one another's, so from that perspective it made total sense for us to team up on this. But some of us have also actually been friends and writing partners for years prior to this. Anyone have a memorable story about how they met any of the other authors here?

JEN: Okay, I know I'm the one who asked this question, but I'm jumping in to answer first! Gail and I have coauthored several books together (the You're Invited series) but I don't know if you guys know that we had only met in person for a single one-hour lunch before we collaborated on those. We actually met online when we entered the same writing contest and—Gail, was it me commenting on yours or you commenting on mine?

GAIL: I can't remember. I think you commenting on mine.

JEN: I think so too. Gail posted the opening to her story and I commented below asking if she'd consider letting me read the whole thing. I'm so greedy for good words!

GAIL: *(Laughs.)* You are. But we quickly became friends and writing partners!

DEE: Jen and I met in a similar way, only I was judging a writing contest and she was one of the entrants. As soon as the contest was over, I went on Twitter and shouted, "Who is this author?! I need to read the rest of her story!" I met everyone else through a mix of Twitter, writing conferences, and this project. Ronni and I are fellow vegetarians, so we bonded when she warned me that there was bacon in the salad at a conference we were both attending.

RONNI: Come to think of it, Jen introduced us at that conference. She's the godmother of all things writing for me! I met Jen on Twitter when I bid on an auction she was hosting. As I was a total newbie, to both writing and Twitter, I didn't think it at all weird that I responded to her tweet asking writer friends where they should have a writer's weekend retreat. They were looking for a house to rent on a lake, in between NY and Boston, and at that time, I just so happened to live in a house on a lake, in between NY and Boston. So naturally, I invited them over for the weekend! Alison, you were one of the writers, so that's when I met you! My husband thought it was totally crazy I was inviting strangers to stay at our house, but you guys didn't feel like strangers at all. And you definitely aren't anymore.

JEN: Ha! I'd forgotten that was our very first time meeting, when I showed up at your door with a suitcase in hand. I ought to try tweeting about looking for an all-expense-paid trip to Australia, just to see what response I get!

Okay, back to the story. Let's tell people about the process we used to write this book together. We had the general concept of a story revolving around a middle school dance, but things really started with one big video call, not unlike this one, to bounce around plot ideas. Who wants to talk about how we picked which characters we'd each write?

STEPH: Someone mentioned there should be a boy. I wrote romance novels way back in the beginning of my career, so I've written at least a dozen novels that included the adult male perspective. However, getting in the mind of an adolescent male is a completely different thing. I'm still not 100 percent sure how teenage boys think, but I definitely know how it feels to be a teenager who likes someone. I tried to combine that with what I know about the differences in the male mind and, voilà, Ryan was born!

RONNI: I thought writing about a character who wouldn't normally be excited about a middle school dance—but this time was—would be interesting. Then we brainstormed the idea of her getting her heart broken in an unexpected way, and I couldn't wait to get inside Ellie's head.

GAIL: We all threw out character suggestions. One of mine was a girl who shows up to the dance only to find out that another girl thinks she has the same date. As we worked together to find ways to tie the main characters to each other, Tess became a member of Heart Grenade (and I honestly can't remember if that was my idea or someone else's!).

(Everyone shrugs.)

JEN: We should have recorded that call for posterity!

RACHELE: I wanted to write about a character who couldn't be at the dance. I remember there were times I couldn't do something my friends were doing and how awful that feeling of being left out was. You think that everyone is having fun without you, and I wanted to create a character who felt that same way. However, Carmen turns out to have a great night, so maybe she was in exactly the right place! Just to add, when we were brainstorming ideas, I came up with a character who Jen wanted to write. So basically I bargained to write Carmen: it went something along the lines of, "Okay, you can use this idea, if I can write a character who isn't at the dance." Nothing like making deals to write the character you want!

JEN: Now that, I definitely remember! I *really* wanted to write the girl who was trying her hardest, despite all kinds of zany obstacles, to get to the dance. And having Ashlyn be a bit bratty (okay, a *lot* bratty) just made it even more fun to be inside her head.

DEE: I remember sitting back and listening to all the great character ideas, but I wasn't sure who mine should be. Once all the others started to come together, I said, "I feel like there should be someone sinister who's there to cause trouble." And I just knew Jade would be fun to write.

JEN: Once we had our characters picked, we each figured out the beginning, middle, and end for our character's dance experience. It just so happened Alison and I were on another writing retreat (sorry, Ronni, we cheated on your lake house) and I remember a chilly afternoon on the back porch—

ALISON: With an entire bag of M&Ms—

JEN: Essential plotting food! We had everyone's beginnings, middles, and ends on separate notecards and we spent hours rearranging them and coming up with a timeline that would work so that each character was in the story somewhat equally and no one disappeared for too long. It was like a giant puzzle. Which leads to the next question . . .

Once we had the outline (derived from those notecards) and a timeline for the events, we each went off to write our own chapters on a pretty tight rotating schedule. For most of us, that's different from how we write our own solo books. What were some of the good and/or bad things about writing this way?

RACHELE: I love that we had a set schedule to follow, so I knew I had to get my chapters written. I can be a bit of procrastinator, so knowing that everyone was depending on me to get my work done was the motivation I needed to, well, get my work done!

ALISON: I've always been really uncomfortable showing unpolished work to other people, and this process forced me to be less precious and perfectionistic about my own words. There just wasn't time to revise a chapter five times before posting it! After a while, it started to feel normal to let people see my work in really early stages, which I think will serve me well in the future!

AN INTERVIEW WITH THE AUTHORS

DEE: Whatever we changed in our own chapters could potentially affect others, so we had to be careful. One of my favorite things was hopping on the phone or having a big e-mail conversation to chat with Ronni, Jen, and Gail so we could figure out how certain plot points with our four connected characters would play out.

RONNI: I loved that we not only worked on our own character's story arc, but also on one another's characters' story arcs, because many of them intersected. That process forced me to look at the bigger picture, rather than focus on one chapter at a time (which is what I usually do when writing alone).

GAIL: I loved having a built-in critique group! And I'm totally the one who was watching people type their chapters in Google docs. Heeheehee.

JEN: Yeah, I learned this about Gail when writing *You're Invited*. She's evil! For me, I really loved going to bed with one chapter written only to wake up and find four more chapters had been added. Oh how I wish my own books wrote themselves while I slept!

AN INTERVIEW WITH THE AUTHORS

Speaking of our own books . . . did anything about writing a story with six other people change your process for writing your solo books?

GAIL: Not necessarily the process, but I've definitely been influenced by spending so much time with everyone else's writing. It's fun to see (and learn from!) everyone's strengths. For example, Dee is a whiz at coming up with pranks. Stephanie actually got into the head of a twelve-year-old boy(!). And Ronni's character is written with so much heart! I've learned so much from everyone in this group.

RACHELE: And don't forget Alison's amazing talent of coming up with band names!!!

JEN: She actually keeps a file of fictional band names on her phone! I've seen it and there lies genius within!

STEPHANIE: I've never been a planner, so working in a highly structured situation was very eye-opening to me. It showed me how much better a book flows when the writer has a chapter-by-chapter outline in hand from the start. I may try that with one of my books to see if I can force myself into "planner" mode!

RACHELE: I agree with Stephanie! Usually when I write my books there are tons of drafts and things often don't go in order or as planned. I always know where I'm heading and how I want the book to end, but I don't always know how my characters get there. My characters surprise me a lot as I follow their journeys, which can be fun, but also stressful at times! I must say that writing to an outline and having everything plotted out is A LOT easier!

Okay, last question. Let's see how much we're willing to humiliate ourselves. Does anyone want to share a favorite memory from a school dance?

GAIL: My mom and my BFF's mom (who were chaperones) busting some moves to Kris Kross's "Jump." So embarrassing then, but hilarious to remember now!

RACHELE: The outfit I wore to my first middle school dance! I really don't know what I was thinking! I had on black combat boots, black tights, jean shorts, a flannel shirt that I tucked in and a hat. I really hope no one has pictures from that dance. I think the fashion police would have arrested me on the spot!

JEN: I definitely have a similar memory. I went full-on Madonna for a seventh grade dance. A million jelly bracelets up my arm and a belt that had a buckle that said "Boy Toy." I thought I was *sooooo* cool!

RONNI: The boy I liked asked me to the winter dance when I was a sophomore in high school. I couldn't wait to go, but a snowstorm that night canceled the dance. Luckily, it was rescheduled for the following week, and I still clearly remember dancing to "Stairway to Heaven." I was so happy that that song is something like eight minutes long!

ALISON: I went to a really small school, and since everyone in my class had known each other since we were tiny, we kind of all thought of one another as slightly annoying siblings. At our eighth grade dance, we were so reluctant to dance with each other that the teachers started handing out quarters to bribe us.

JEN: We should have included "bribery to dance" in *Best. Night. Ever.*! Alison, you held out on us!! In all seriousness, guys, I know we're talking about school dance memories, but my favorite school dance memory is now, officially, writing about this one at Lynnfield Middle . . . and not just because I got to attend it in hedgehog pj's instead of death-trap heels and a Boy Toy belt. Just like the best dances (and the best nights) ever, it wouldn't have been the same without great friends to share it with! Giant, squishy hugs all around. Um, except online ones, because we're not in the same room.

(Giant, online squishy hugs commence. . . .)

ABOUT THE AUTHORS

RACHELE ALPINE is the author of the middle grade novels *Operation Pucker Up* and *You Throw Like a Girl* and the young adult novels *A Void the Size of the World* and *Canary*. By day she's a high school English teacher, by night she's a wife and mom, and she finds any time in between to write. She lives in Cleveland, Ohio where she writes with the companionship of the world's cutest dog and a big bag of gummy peaches. She loves hearing from readers, and you can find her at rachelealpine.com.

RONNI ARNO is the author of the middle-grade novels *Ruby Reinvented*, *Dear Poppy*, and forthcoming *Molly in the Middle*.

She lives on the coast of Maine with her husband, two daughters, and her dogs, Hazel and Mabel. When she's not writing, Ronni stalks her kids for story ideas, kayaks, and eats chocolate . . . but not usually at the same time. You can visit Ronni at ronniarno.com.

ALISON CHERRY is the author of the middle grade novels *Willows vs. Wolverines* and *The Classy Crooks Club* and the young adult novels *Red*, *For Real*, and *Look Both Ways*. She is a professional photographer and spent many years working as a lighting designer for theater, dance, and opera productions. She lives in Brooklyn, NY with her two cats. Visit her online at alisoncherrybooks.com.

STEPHANIE FARIS knew she wanted to be an author from a very young age. In fact, her mother often told her to stop reading so much and go outside and play with the other kids. After graduating from Middle Tennessee State University she somehow found herself working in information technology. But she never stopped writing. Her middle-grade novels include *30 Days of No Gossip* and *25 Roses*, and she's also the author of the Piper Morgan chapter book series. When she isn't crafting fiction,

ABOUT THE AUTHORS

Stephanie works as a freelance writer for a wide variety of websites and magazines. She lives in Nashville with her husband. Visit her online at stephaniefaris.com.

JEN MALONE once spent a year traveling the world solo, met her husband on the highway (literally), and went into labor with her identical twins while on a rock star's tour bus. These days she saves the drama for her books. Jen's middle-grade novels include *The Sleepover, At Your Service* and forthcoming *The Art of the Swap*, as well as the You're Invited series, co-written with Gail Nall. She has also written the young adult novels *Map to the Stars, Wanderlost,* and *Changes in Latitude.* You can learn more about Jen and her books at jenmalonewrites.com.

GAIL NALL lives in Louisville, Kentucky, with her family and more cats than necessary. She once drove a Zamboni, has camped in the snow in June, and almost got trampled in Paris. Gail is the author of the middle grade novels *Out of Tune, Breaking the Ice,* and *You're Invited* and *You're Invited Too,* written with Jen Malone. She has also written the young adult novel *Exit Stage Left.* You can find her online at gailnall.com.

ABOUT THE AUTHORS

DEE ROMITO lives in her hometown of Buffalo, New York. You're likely to find her on adventures with her husband and two energetic kids, at the local ice cream shop, or curled up in a comfy chair with her cats. She loves to write, travel, and giggle like a teenager with her friends. Dee is the author of the middle-grade novels *The BFF Bucket List* and forthcoming *No Place Like Home*. You can visit her online at deeromito.com.